PRAI

MW01146414

"If this is how the world ends, sign me up!" --Jonathan Maberry, New York Times Best-Selling author of *Patient Zero*

"One of the best zombie novels of the year." -- Paul "Goat" Allen, Barnes & Noble

"Long, a prolific horror author writes with graphic glee--repulsive details and way off-color jokes abound." -- *Tacoma News Tribune*

Other books by
Timothy W. Long

Beyond the Barriers (Permuted Press)
Among the Living (Permuted Press)
Among the Dead (Permuted Press)
At the Behest of the Dead
The Zombie Wilson Diaries
The Apocalypse and Satan's Glory Hole
w/ Jonathan MoOn
Dr. Spengle vs. The Unihorn Horror
w/ Jonathan MoOn
Z-Risen: Outbreak
Z-Risen: Outcasts
Z-Risen: Poisoned Earth

Coming Soon
Impact Earth: First Wave
Z-Risen 4: Reavers

Z-Risen 3:
Poisoned Earth

BY

Timothy W. Long

This one's dedicated to the writers who keep me endlessly entertained and make amazing drinking buddies:
Craig DiLouie, Jonathan Moon, Cheryl Dyson, Peter Clines, Eloise J. Knapp, and of course, Katie Cord.

Credits
Edited by Melodie Ladner
Cover art: Eloise J. Knapp

In the event this log is found with my corpse, I'm Machinist Mate First Class Jackson Creed and it's been a week since we arrived back in San Diego following the event. With me is Marine Sergeant Joel "Cruze" Kelly.

We were both stationed on the USS McClusky, an Oliver Hazard Perry-class frigate out of San Diego. Our ship was overrun by the dead and we barely escaped with our lives. Now we live in the middle of Undead Central.

###

Z-Risen 3: Poisoned Earth

SSDD

05:35 hours approximate
Location: Just outside of L.A.

The sun rose over a desolate road, and that's the nicest thing I could say about the morning.

Abandoned cars and trucks lay across the road like an obstacle course in hell. Suitcases had been emptied and tossed to the side. Glove boxes hung loose and had long since been vacated of all but papers and melted tubes of lipstick. I no longer bothered to check under seats.

After a vehicle had sat in the sun for a few weeks, anything that had been edible became something mushy and frequently sported mold or, as a real bonus, maggots and rot. I once found a bag with a freaking severed hand inside. The hand didn't move, but I damn sure did. What kind of a wacko cuts off someone's hand and leaves it in a goddamn bag?

There was enough debris littering the road to remind me of a war documentary. I used to watch the History Channel. They always showed men

9

and women on the move, dragging kids and belongings. That wasn't the case now. We were in the midst of a full-scale war that none of us were truly equipped to deal with. We did our best, but it was hard to handle the shitstorm we'd endured for the past month.

The level of Zs had decreased as we moved away from the city on our journey to Los Angeles. That didn't mean we could be any less vigilant. One wrong move--one careless step like forgetting to check under the camper before everyone was out--and it could be the end for one or all of us.

I'd seen a Z try to grab Christy when she dropped to the ground. Either we'd run over the bastard or he'd crawled under there during the night. He'd sent Christy stumbling back and screaming. I wasn't too quick with the wrench, because bashing something that's got its head under a vehicle is like the most fucked up game of Whack-A-Mole ever devised.

Just another day in paradise.

The night before, we'd spent our time huddled in the camper, backed up between two houses so we had an easy exit. The pair of ramblers was so close together that the truck slid between them, leaving very little room on either side of our mobile home. If the Zs came, we'd have a fighting chance.

Following our escape from a shitload of shufflers and an asshole with an army, we'd spent a week plus change on the road. We didn't move all that fast. Didn't try to. It was a time to lick our wounds and press on. Los Angeles had become some kind of quest. It was our fiery mountain in Mordor. It was where we'd find warm beds, food, and acceptance. We had talked about it so much and for so long we no longer considered what would happen if the town was like everywhere else we'd visited: fucked.

Frosty--our newly adopted dog--was the only one that played it cool. She nosed around the little camper, and I took her out when she sniffed at the door. She always kept on guard, and still didn't bark when Zs were near. I was tempted on more than one occasion to let her tease some Zs like she'd done the day I found her. Seemed like she loved nothing more than taunting the undead and leading them on a chase. But she was also smart enough not to let one of the rotters get ahold of her.

When I went out, Christy went with me, and hung around asking questions every minute. Never knew a kid could have so many random thoughts in her head. When will we find a place to sleep? Where are we going to get some fresh fruit? Could we grow a garden somewhere? Would I ever tell Anna how I felt about her? That last one got me, but I ignored it, because Anna was aloof about what had happened between us. Two could play that game, so I kept my mouth shut for a change.

When we found our safe place for the night,

Christy took Frosty out to play. With the dog outside, I knew that if she got a whiff of more than one or two Zs she'd sound the alarm and we'd hightail it to a new hiding spot.

#

07:20 hours approximate
Location: Vista

Joel had spent a couple of days sitting around looking miserable while we all did our best not to get on each other's nerves. Bunch of hardasses in a tiny space meant tempers could quickly flare. One time I was so sick of being cooped up with them, I took a walk just to clear my head. Cleared my guts, too, because I had hellacious gas. If it was just me and Joel, we'd fart and play it off, give each other an earful and then look for a window to open. But Anna and Roz had this way of looking at us like we were a couple of thirteen-year-olds.

It was so early the crickets were still making a hell of a lot of noise. I'd been outside stretching my legs when I'd realized that the new world had a weird smell. Fresh and clean. Kinda ironic considering all the dead stuff we'd seen over the last few months. After I found a place to piss, I headed back to the camper so we could gather around the small table and plan our next move.

Anna rested on the edge of the bed. Her arm was a mess from the gunshot wound. Roz sat in the tiny alcove, curved in a display of terrible posture, one knee cocked back and her other leg under the table. Christy was trying to teach Frosty to hold a treat on her nose until she was given the command to eat it. The treat was just some dried-out food from the night before. Frosty thought it was the shit, but didn't seem to think much of the game.

Joel stood over the table like a limp-dick general. His ebony skin was sallow. After taking a couple of rounds to his IMTV armor he'd been left bruised and battered. We'd had a hell of a fight on our hands.

Now, a week of rest had done little but irritate him. We studied a beat-up map of the area, looking to stick to any roads that were off the main drag.

This plan didn't always work out so well. Looking at a map was one thing. Actually finding our way was another. We'd pick a side road, head toward a larger road, and then learn the hard way that "progress" had screwed up anything resembling what we found on our fifteen-year-old paper map. One thing the zombie fucking apocalypse did not allow for was GPS.

The day before, Roz and I had raided a little convenience store. Miraculously, the place had only been mostly picked over. We found some dried goods, but not so much in the canned food department. Roz did turn up one of the most disgusting things I've ever seen in my life: a whole cooked chicken in a can. When that abortion slid out of the tin, I thought I was going to puke up all the stomach acid my empty gut had to offer.

It'd tasted worse than it looked. It was so bad I dreamed of some mid-rats back on the McClusky; that stuff tasted like boiled shoe leather, but beggars can't be choosers. You either get used to eating shitty food or you starve. You get used to being on the run, constantly looking over your shoulder. You get used to the moans and groans of Zs. You get used to hiding and keeping quiet. If you don't, it's a quick trip to zombieville.

And that's why I'd choked the stuff down and been thankful for the protein.

Frosty had nosed around, so I ripped off a few ounces and fed her. She licked my fingers and whined for more.

"I know, dude. Good shit." I rubbed her head.

A half hour later we'd headed back to the camper where we shared the meager contents from our backpacks. Roz had inspected Anna's wound and "tsked" a few times. She then took a turn feeling up Joel's chest to check for cracked or broken ribs. She told him the bruising and swelling were going down.

"Hear that, jarhead? You're going to be around for a while, so suck it up," I'd grinned.

"I got something you can suck," Joel had shot back, and grabbed his crotch, but winced for the effort.

When McQuinn's army of jackwads had tried to take us down, we'd concocted a stupid plan that involved leading an army of Zs right at the other guys. Joel had made use of an ambulance, complete with flashing lights and a siren that told all of southern California we were still alive. The ambulance had crashed, and that's when he'd been shot. His armor had saved his life, but it hadn't saved him from looking like he'd been punched repeatedly by a gorilla.

"Get some rest, Joel," Roz had advised. He'd rolled his eyes at me, so I'd shrugged and gone back to staring out of the space between the curtain and the window. I'd expected a horde of undead to locate us at any moment and make our lives hell.

To be clear, I expect this from every moment of every day.

"I'm fine. Just got the wind knocked out of me," Joel had said.

"Fuck's sake, Joel. It's like you got kicked in the chest by a donkey. Just chill and stop being a jarhead for a day," I'd said.

"Yeah. You say that now. Wait till your ass is hanging in the wind and a bunch of ZULUs are about to take a bite," Joel had said.

"I'll keep that in mind, and I'll keep my ass pointed in your direction."

Joel hadn't said anything and instead, started to field-strip his assault rifle for what seemed like the twentieth time. Of all the weapons we'd had along the way, Joel had never abandoned the Rock River Arms AR-15 with its EOTech holographic sight. He loved it like it was his own rotten little kid. When he thought he'd lost it during a firefight, he'd made us go back a few days later and scour the area for the gun.

08:35 hours approximate
Location: Vista

The next few days passed in a blur. We stayed a tight group for the most part, but being a tight group meant that we were together too much and for too long. We laughed, bickered, fought, and had to keep more than one screaming match down to more of a hissing match so the Zs didn't hear us. Joel and I had been cooped up together for days at a time, but we'd developed a way to deal with it: just not talking to each other. With a teenage girl and two women in our group, it wasn't that easy.

I think it was a Thursday when we decided that we'd have to range out in a wider area to find a cache of supplies. I hated it, but we were going to have to hit some houses. That was dangerous. Open a door and there could be a Z waiting to pounce. Knock on a door and there could be a civilian waiting to shoot. And houses weren't our only worry. We hadn't seen a shuffler in days. Instead of being reassuring, it scared the shit out of me.

The shufflers were smart and cunning. They weren't like regular Zs, because they seemed to be able to think. Not only that, but they acted in groups and were able to hide in masses of Zs.

But that wasn't the real reason. Anna had a bullet in her arm, and as much as she'd played it off--and even though Roz had cleaned the wound and told us everything was okay--Anna was hot. She'd had a low-grade fever for a couple of days. We needed to get the bullet out, and Roz said she needed antibiotics.

So I counted rounds, readied gear, and then lay next to Anna for the night. She slept like a rock, but it was a long time before I dropped off.

06:10 hours approximate
Location: Vista

Morning arrived like a bitch with a hangover. I rolled over, studied the light streaming in from the outside world, and thought about taking a siesta for the rest of the week. Let the others do supply runs. I was sick of it. Running, hiding, ducking, sneaking, and bashing in heads. Wears a guy down, you know?

After I quit feeling sorry for myself, I became aware that Anna had backed up against me in the night. I had one arm over her waist and she was snuggled right against my chest with her head resting on my arm. My hand had fallen asleep but I didn't care to move it. She smelled good. Feminine.

When it was time to do the supply run, I tried one last time to tell Joel to take it easy and take care of his wounds. Joel flatly responded that he and I were going out there. I nodded. Besides, if we had to spend another day holed up in this tiny camper, I was going to go fucking postal.

Joel said he was better and Roz seemed to agree.

"I'll take it any way I can get it," he said.

Roz looked like she wanted to punch him in the face.

Joel had gone over his IMTV tactical gear and made adjustments. He'd tossed out a shattered ceramic piece of armor that had saved his life, then twiddled with other pieces until his chest was protected. After the battle at the RV camp, we were dangerously low on ammo. I took Anna's Smith & Wesson R8 .357. She glowered at me but I promised to bring her boyfriend back.

"Don't lose him," she said.

"I meant me," I said and tried to pull off a cool smirk-wink thing. All I got in return was a flat look.

We had an assortment of 9mm pistols, but barely enough ammo to fill all the magazines. Joel settled on the Beretta 92FS and stuffed a handful of extra rounds into his pockets. He had nearly a full magazine for AR-15. Joel slipped the mag into a pouch, snapped his assault rifle onto a two-point sling and draped it around his body.

During scouting missions, food runs, and house invasions we'd come up with so many different types of guns it was hard to keep track. I was happy with my Springfield XDM compact and always kept it close.

I hoped we had enough ammo to get us out of a scrape.

I took my trusty wrench and draped it over my shoulder. I'd found a piece of webbing that had been a guitar strap, and constructed a half-assed strap for the weapon. The wrench was conveniently left to swing under my arm, but it banged against my hip and side with every step. I had to figure out a better way to carry this thing, or leave it behind. But if there was one lesson I'd learned over the last three weeks, it was to never go unarmed. Never.

"Think we should bring Frosty?" I asked Joel.

"I don't know. What if we get stuck and have to hide out for a day or two? How we going to keep her from going stir crazy?"

"How am I going to keep *you* from going stir crazy? Put a jarhead in a box and shit gets busted and shot up," I said.

Joel snorted, but eyed Frosty.

"I don't know, man."

"Just leave her with Christy. She loves the girl

more than me anyway."

"Because I'm cute and you smell like a sweaty guy," Christy said.

"You smell like sweat too. You just can't tell," I teased.

Christy looked at me like I'd slapped her.

"I do not stink! And it's not like I can take a bath unless you can bring back a barrel of water."

"I'm sorry, dude," I tried. "I was just teasing. You smell like roses and puppy dog farts."

"You're so gross, Creed," she said with a laugh.

Frosty nudged Christy's side, and got her head rubbed for the effort.

"We'll leave her here," I nodded at Frosty. "Hear that, dog? You're on guard duty."

Frosty didn't answer but she did loll her pink tongue out of the side of her mouth.

Roz said she'd stay behind and keep an eye on Anna and Christy. Better her than me. She handed me a list of usable antibiotics and told me to be on the lookout for them.

I'd been stuffed into this fucking sardine can for days and I needed a break. I needed fresh air, even if that air reeked of the Zs. With quick goodbyes that included me unsuccessfully trying to kiss Anna Sails on the cheek, we left.

We'd walked a few minutes when Joel broke the silence.

"Sails doesn't seem to like you much."

"What, that? She just doesn't like public displays of affection."

"She tell you that?" He raised his eyebrows.

"I figured it out."

"Lotta figuring with that girl," he said.

"Tell me about it."

09:00 hours approximate
Location: Vista

We followed a well-worn path down concrete lanes littered with--you guessed it--more fucking trash, and the remains of whatever had been inside shops and houses. There was enough empty luggage to fill an abandoned Kohl's. Joel was not much of a conversationalist while we made the trek toward town.

Someone had painted a mural of zombies eating a couple of children. The piece of art was complete with heads smashed in and brains leaking onto the ground.

"Worst graffiti I've seen in my life," I muttered.

A shape flashed across an alley and faded into shadow. Joel followed it with his gun but didn't start blasting, so I didn't either. I'd learned a great rule from Marine Sergeant Joel "Cruze" Kelly, and that was not to start firing until after he started firing.

When he finally unlocked his gaze from the alley, I took a step and accidentally kicked over a can. It clattered across the ground and landed next to the sidewalk. Joel froze and swept his gun up.

Luckily, a dozen Zs didn't descend on us.

"Fuck is wrong with you?"

"What? I didn't see it," I said.

"How could you miss a big empty can of Campbell's soup sitting right in the middle of the walkway, man?"

"Because I'm taller than you and that gun put together."

Something moved in the alley again so I took a step toward it. I crunched over someone's cheap bead jewelry and a pile of soggy trash. I couldn't tell who was moving around back there, and curiosity was getting the better of me. The shape faded into shadow after I caught a glimpse of someone dressed in black complete with a ski mask to up the creep factor.

I got the chills just seeing the guy. If someone was stalking us I'd prefer that me and Joel do our talking with guns or fists.

"Bad hombres. Let's move out," Joel said.

I agreed with him and followed.

It was 0900 hours and I hadn't seen a Z since the day before.

It felt fucking eerie.

Gold Mine

09:40 hours approximate
Location: Vista

The Z hit me like a ton of bricks.

My partner in crime yelled for me to move out of the way, but I was slow on my feet. We'd come across a group of feisty assholes about fifteen minutes ago and ducked into the remains of an ampm. He and I huddled for a few minutes, but the sounds of something moving in the back of the convenience store finally got under my skin.

The Z had been hovering near a shelf, and no more than a few feet away. In the gloom I didn't even see him until his shuffling steps betrayed him. He moved fast, arms up, milky white gaze locked on my face like it was prime rib. I spun, and panic made me lose my cool. That's when the Z almost got a piece of my dumb ass.

I hit the wall hard enough to see stars. Breath whooshed out but I got my hands up, purely by instinct, and fought off the Z. He had about fifty pounds on me and slammed me right back into the wall. I pushed the Z away. Something clamped my wrist and I squealed like a six year old.

It wasn't teeth, it was his hand. Most of his fingers had been gnawed to the bone, and he had a hell of a death grip. I got my foot up and kicked the zombie in the chest. He fell away but his hand was still fastened to me. That's when I noticed he'd fallen away, all except his arm. I bounced around like I was in a one-man idiot dance-off as I tried to shake it loose.

Joel was fast on his feet, just like I'd expected. If a Marine wasn't shooting stuff, punching stuff, or just snarling at stuff, he was probably asleep while standing up, expecting an attack at any second.

He grabbed the zombie by the collar and knocked him to the ground. Joel lifted his boot and brought it down on the Z's head once, twice, and then a third time that left pulp leaking from the man's cracked skull. The Z didn't move again.

I leaned over and tried to catch my breath. Hands on knees, chest spasming as I sucked in air.

"Need a hand?" Joel nodded at the Z's appendage that was still stuck to my arm.

"Oh that's real funny," I said.

Fuck! It really was stuck on there. I flailed around, trying to shake it off.

"Looks like he had a strong grip," Joel deadpanned.

"Okay, that's enough," I said, and mostly meant it. I was worried that if I actually caught my breath I'd break into laughter.

The arm refused to let go and as I shook it, bits of blood and flesh flew. Joel moved out of the way of the little projectiles.

"You're giving shaking hands a new meaning, man."

"I hate this fucking place."

"Your ability to state the obvious is a **real gift**, Creed." Joel smacked my shoulder, lifted his assault rifle and moved toward the back of the store. I grabbed the remains of the arm and pulled it free, and left it next to the Z's battered body.

More movement in the rear of the store meant that my little break was over.

Joel held up a hand to motion me to stay put. I did just that, trusting that he was confident enough to take on whatever was creeping around. From the soft scraping, I hoped it was just a torso looking for a meal.

A few weeks ago that shit used to get to me. Seeing bodies or halves of bodies still crawling around used to freak me out so bad I wouldn't sleep for days. Now it was just another sun-up in Undead Central US of A. The Zs had lost their souls or whatever made them thinking and reasoning beings, leaving them as brainless meat bags capable of little more than piss-hate coupled with an appetite for human flesh.

I've learned, thanks to the walking **Marine hard-on named Sergeant Kelly,** to be more aware of my surroundings. Don't let the above Z attack fool you. I'm a lean (because I haven't had a proper meal in days), mean (because I haven't had a proper meal in days), killing machine (you get the goddamn picture).

I noticed that the little store reeked of spoiled food, rotting flesh, and blood when we sniffed around the entrance, but give a squid a break for hoping for a bag of Doritos.

Turned out the shelves were bare and probably had been for days. Mom and Pop stores had been well-defended at the start of the damn apocalypse, but then the looters had gotten into it.

Guys like Frank McQuinn, who just over a week ago had led his merry band of jackholes against my group and a bunch of retirees who wanted to be left to their own meandering devices. We'd hurt McQuinn and his group and they'd scattered. The quick brains of Kelly and my girl, Anna Sails, had saved us. Now she was stuck in a camper with a bullet in her arm and I was out trying to find supplies to fix her up.

A pair of shapes slid behind a shelf. Joel motioned for me to take the other side. I moved away from him, head low, shoulders hunched, eyes on the floor as I sought out anything that might make noise like an errant Funyun or potato chip. If I saw one I would likely start drooling, then it would be a struggle to stop from eating it. Was there such a thing as "the three or four week rule"?

I met Joel's eyes. He nodded and we swung around the shelving from opposite sides.

My wrench was already in hand and I'd raised it, preparing to bash in at least one head, all the while hoping that Joel wouldn't shoot my ass off.

I nearly jumped out of my skin when the little figures dashed into view.

The kids were filthy and had to be a lot younger than Christy. A pair of boys, just little kids really, with faces covered in dirt, hair a rats-nest, clothes holed and hanging in strips. My first impulse was to swing the wrench, because they looked like Zs.

"We ain't like those things," one of the kids said.

"We're just looking for water or food," the other said.

Joel blew out a breath and pointed his gun toward the floor.

"You dudes got family?" I asked.

"Yeah. Right outside the door," one of them said.

They were on the move before I could ask who was waiting for them. The kids were fast and slipped away and out the front before I could get another word in.

"Well shit," Joel said.

"Hey! Come back!" I called and moved toward the door.

I poked my head out, but they were gone. I

could probably pursue them, but the little rug rats were a lot faster than me. Besides, what was I going to do when I caught up with them? More than likely they did have someone around here watching after them. Someone with a big ass gun, and a bullet labeled "Jackson Creed".

I stopped scanning for them when I noticed a shape across the street. He was dressed in black from head to toe with only his eyes peering through some kind of ski-mask-looking thing. This had to be the guy I'd seen earlier in the day.

The person had a big assault rifle at the ready, so I slowly raised my hands to show I didn't feel like getting shot today. If that was one of McQuinn's guys, I was probably wasting my time and should plant my gut on the ground.

Another **figure** appeared next to the first and I could have sworn one of them nodded in my direction. Then they both faded from view.

10:10 hours approximate
Location: Vista

We moved out a few minutes later. I kept my eyes peeled but I never saw the two figures again. I tried to convince myself that they'd been a figment of my imagination.

We came across decaying corpses, most unmoving. Whenever we did find a Z, we quickly assessed its threat level, and ended up leaving the majority of them behind. If any got too jumpy, a quick swing of my wrench put them down for good. They were a sorry bunch even for zombies. Most had taken damage of some kind and were no longer up and moving around.

A particularly enthusiastic female--in her fifties, if I had to guess, hard to tell with the crushed face and shattered eye socket--pursued us with one working arm and one working leg. Her other limbs had been shattered like someone had dropped her from twenty feet up.

After a while it was just pathetic, and so I also put her out of her misery.

A telephone pole had a hand-printed sign nailed to it. I moved closer and read. Joel covered for me while I shook my head. After considering the words, I pulled the sheet off and showed Joel.

"Think this is real?"

"Sounds no good to me, brother," Joel said while rubbing his chin with one hand.

"But what if it's true?"

"I'm not sure I want to find out."

I nodded and stuffed the flyer in my backpack.

Every store we came across had been picked over. We finally got lucky when we started to boldly bust in doors on houses. Risking noise, because I was a little out of my mind with worry over Anna, we ransacked three houses in a row, killed the undead inhabitants, and taken everything that wasn't nailed down. A three-quarters eaten box of stale Ritz crackers. Some beef jerky that didn't amount to much more than a taste for both of us. I found a can of chicken broth. I couldn't wait. I broke out my can opener and punched a pair of holes in the aluminum, then Joel and I took turns drinking like it was a fifteen-dollar bottle of whiskey.

"This won't last," Joel observed.

"What?"

"The houses with goods. As more and more get picked over we'll be coming up empty on our supply runs."

"These are mostly picked over *now*. Guess we better stock up while we can. We have the camper, it can hold a lot of food."

"Yeah, but five people can *eat* a lot of food. *You* eat enough for *three* people."

"I don't eat that much. Shit, man, I've lost enough weight to look like a college basketball player. Look at this trim and fit example of military bearing."

"You look like you should be going into rehab. Like a damn crackhead."

"Yeah, well *you* look like you should be on a milk carton."

"The fuck does that even mean?" Joel asked.

"I don't know. I'm tired, man. Brain ain't up to sparring with you today."

Joel looked me up and down. "You're alright. Let's get this shit over with so we can lounge around in robes and sip espresso while Roz and Anna feed us grapes."

"Anna's more likely to feed me the barrel of a gun."

Joel snorted and moved out.

We dashed across a street littered with all kinds of crap that had been left behind, or tossed aside as people realized they were more likely to live if they were mobile. Bodies lay here and there, but no biters rose to greet us.

We checked out a house that was missing its door, and after hearing an awful lot of banging around on the second floor, decided to try somewhere else.

We moved between a pair of apartment complexes and found a group of Zs milling around. They were lethargic and dressed in tatters. Joel and I backed up, but one of them got its eyes on us. It lurched toward me, but it was barely ambulatory. I took it out and then the one behind it. Joel used the stock of his gun to smack Zs down and I finished them off.

"Why are they so messed up?" I asked.

"Fucking zombies, man," Joel said.

"No shit, but they were a mess even for Zs."

"Maybe they been decaying. Old Zs," Joel said. "Give 'em another week and they might be crawling. A week after that they might just stop moving."

"What if they all get old and slow? Think the shufflers will slow down?"

"Don't know, brother. I'm too tired to worry about it right now."

###

10:50 hours approximate
Location: Vista

The next home was a goldmine.

The house we'd picked was a single story with three bedrooms. The last door on the left was closed and I thought I'd heard something thumping around in there, so we didn't bother exploring that room.

There was a huge bloodstain on the carpet leading into the dining room, but we couldn't find a body to go with it. Didn't matter anyway. After a couple of weeks of this shitty new life, I was just about immune to the horrors. I might have been squeamish at one time. I might have looked away when a doctor cut into my finger to sew a tendon back together. Now it was different. A guy with his guts hanging out, half his face eaten away, and dragging a broken foot, was just another day in undead central.

I hit the bathroom while Joel tossed the kitchen. I needed to piss, and got lucky and didn't find a mess in the toilet. Sure, I can pick any corner of the world to take a leak in, but it didn't hurt to pretend to be civilized from time to time.

I opened drawers and came up with a bottle of Percocets that had expired a year ago. There was a bottle of TUMS, so I ate a few for the calcium. I found some birth control pills, considered them, and decided to leave the packet. It was better than getting slapped in the face by Anna Sails.

"Oh yay. Jackpot, baby," Joel called from the other room.

I followed his voice into the hallway. He was rifling through a pantry, and he wasn't being very organized about it. Open boxes were tossed to one side, while cans and closed supplies were put on the other side.

"What?" I asked.

"Found this," he said and held up a flat box.

"That looks like a pan or something," I said.

"Nah, man. It's a burner. Takes these little cans of butane. You can even use it inside and it won't kill ya."

"Nifty," I said.

"No more digging a fire pit and hoping we aren't sniffed out. As long as we have fuel we can cook inside." Joel grinned and pushed the box into his backpack along with a bunch of cans that looked like old-school hairspray.

I wasn't as excited as Joel. I'd gotten used to eating stuff right out of cans and cold. Chicken noodle soup wasn't half bad in a congealed form. It filled the gut and was easy to open and consume.

In the bedroom I tossed the contents of a nightstand and came across a half bottle of something with a name so long I wasn't about to try to pronounce it. I added it to the bag, along with a full bottle of antidepressants. Too bad there wasn't enough to keep us all medicated for a year. If I was going to spend all of my time shooting Zs, I'd love to do it with a smile on my face.

I also found a pair of fuzzy handcuffs.

"Kinky bastard," Joel said. I hadn't even heard him moving down the hallway.

"Antidepressants and handcuffs. Ain't that some shit," I laughed.

"Place must have belonged to white people," Joel said, and went to check out the last bedroom.

I went through a dresser and found enough silky lingerie to open a Victoria's Secret store. I held up a pair of flimsy, see-through panties and squinted. "Why not?" I muttered and stuffed a few items in the bottom of my backpack.

"Shit yeah." Joel said from the other room.

He'd put a dresser drawer on the bed and was busy sorting out ammo. Whoever had lived here had been ready for action. It made me wonder where they were now.

"Box of nine. Seven boxes of forty. Damn, we should check for that piece. And look at this. A few boxes of .45 rounds. Dude had a fucking armory. I love whoever lived here."

"You could tell him. He's probably the fucker thumping around in the last bedroom."

"If at all possible, let's avoid looking in that room. Could be another shuffler-kid, I'd rather just leave it a mystery."

"Good thing those smart Zs can't figure out the complexities of a doorknob," I said. "Reminds me of the aliens in that movie *Signs*. They traveled a million light years to conquer earth but couldn't open a damn door."

I pulled out more drawers and felt underneath clothing. I opened the closet and took down boxes and moved hangers around.

"I think some of this will fit your girlish figure," I said, and tossed a few button-down shirts at Joel.

"I always wanted to wear shirts decorated with little alligators," Joel said.

"No gun. We might have to open the last door."

"Check under the mattress," Joel said.

"Genius," I nodded.

I slid the mattress to the side and found something that made my eyes light up.

Underneath, we'd hit the jackpot.

The .40 was a Smith & Wesson sized for conceal and carry. There was an extra magazine with an extended grip that would hold a few extra rounds. The gun was already loaded, and the second mag also contained a long row of rounds.

Next to the .40 was a weird-looking assault rifle. Joel went around to the other side of the mattress, and together we lifted it and put it against the wall.

"Holy fuckballs," I said.

"This isn't a bed, it's a damn armory."

There was a hunting rifle, a double barrel shotgun, and an assortment of knives. There was even a broad-bladed sword in a scabbard. I picked up the long weapon and pulled the blade out a few inches. Steel gleamed back at me.

"Look at this thing."

"You finally found a hand weapon more impressive than the wrench."

"I'll stick with my metal club," I said. I didn't know the first thing about wielding a sword and didn't want to learn while Zs were on the attack. I'd probably be just as dangerous to Joel as to the Zs if I started swinging the blade around.

Joel picked up the rifle and looked it over. He popped the magazine out and looked inside.

"That's wild."

"What?"

"Sig MPX. It fires .40 caliber rounds. That explains all the ammo."

"Is that weird?"

"Nah. Probably good for home defense. Stock slides in to make it a pistol. See that short barrel? You can make a burglar regret every syllable in 'breaking and entering'. I'll have to test it to see if it has any kind of range. Might not be too accurate."

I shrugged and started stuffing ammo into my backpack. We didn't find any shotgun ammo, which was a shame. I'd have loved to sling the double barrel over my back. I missed the Mossberg tactical shotgun I'd lost during the battle at the RV park.

We'd been in the house for longer than I liked. The first week of the event had seen us planning for fights and timing them. If it took more than thirty seconds to take down Zs, we'd just haul ass. That was before the shufflers had become so prevalent. Our raiding time had been two minutes: in and out, squeaky-clean. See some Zs? Just move out and find another home.

Now we were almost leisurely, and that was going to get dangerous. I thought about telling Joel that we needed to move with a purpose, but he'd been quiet about how badly he was hurt, so I didn't push him.

Joel ripped a case off a pillow and stuffed it with boxes of rounds. He didn't bother with the knives, and I tossed the sword back on the mattress. The next group of survivors could have them.

Joel moved into the hallway and I was right behind him. I paused to listen at the closed door. I pressed my ear right up against the particle board and listened.

"Nothing," I whispered.

Something hit the door so hard it rattled in its frame. I jumped back, barely covering a curse.

"Like a peeping Tom with your pants around your ankles. Okay, I'm calling it," Joel said.

I nodded sheepishly.

We stopped in the kitchen on our way out for a last look around.

Someone had cleaned before they left. I could almost picture a family moving around, thinking that the worst would be over soon, that they'd be back in their house in a day, maybe two.

We grabbed canned goods and even a box of crackers. I found an opened can of Easy Cheese in the back of a pantry.

"Know how bad I want to squirt half that can into my mouth?" I asked Joel. "Reminds me of a few months ago when supplies were more abundant. I think we found some of this gas inducing crap back then."

"I know about you squids and squirting stuff in your mouths," Joel said with a half-smile.

"We learn from the best." I winked at Joel and went back to stuffing goods into my beat-up backpack.

"Nasty ass Sailor."

I leaned my head back and squirted some of the cheese into my mouth anyway. Then I tossed the can at Joel. He laughed at the look on my face, which was probably something like a cross between food-ecstasy and an O face. Stuff tasted so good I wanted to take it on a date and ask it to move in.

Joel tossed the can back, so I went ahead and finished it off. I'd pay for it later as it hit my gut, but it was worth it for now.

With our packs full and our bellies no longer rumbling, Joel moved to the hallway and stared at the last door on the right.

"No, man."

"What if there's something in there that we can use? These assholes had a lot of food and guns. Maybe there's a bottle of Viagra in that room with your name on it," Joel said.

"Let's just go. They need us." I was trying to keep my head on, but we'd been away from the camper for a few hours and I was worried.

"Keep it cool. We're headed back to the rest of the crew."

"I know. I'm just worried about Anna. She's got a bullet in her arm and I'm worried that it may already be infected, for all I know."

Joel put his hand on my shoulder.

"We got this, brother."

I shrugged his hand off my shoulder and opened a few more cabinets. I found dishes and cups, but nothing to eat. On impulse I grabbed a shaker filled with meat seasoning and added it to my collection. Joel stalked down the hallway and listened at the door, and then when something thumped, he returned.

"Curiosity is killing me, Creed, but you're right. Let's call it and get back," he said.

First damn thing Joel had said today that actually made sense.

He moved toward the door.

"Joel, want me to take some of that gear?"

"I'm good."

"You don't look good. You look like you're in pain."

"Just weakness leaving the body, man," he said.

He opened the door and peeked outside.

I'd done my best to string anything that didn't

fit in my backpack around my waist and over my back. The little home defense machine gun rode next to the wrench. We didn't have time to sit around and load it, and neither one of us wanted to contemplate leaving leave it behind.

Joel stepped into the street and then immediately ran back inside. A pair of figures pushed into the doorway after him.

I had my wrench raised, ready to bash heads, when one of them raised a hand.

"No. Wait," a voice with a strong eastern European accent said.

"Civilians, Creed, and we're about to have company."

"Many come," the man said.

The couple were probably in their mid to late thirties. He had a craggy face, with early frown lines and dark skin. She was slight, with a huge blast of curly black hair that surrounded her head like a big halo. She wore a pair of thick-rimmed glasses and a bright yellow rain slicker. I stared at the loud jacket.

"Keep zombie bites out," she said.

"Smart," I said.

"Fall back. We need to find another way out of this place," Joel said.

"How many?" I asked.

"Oh, about a hundred," Joel said, and stormed down the hallway.

"We help?" the man asked.

"I don't know, can you?" I asked.

Don't judge me. It's the zombie fucking apocalypse. I'm all for helping my fellow man, but they have to be able to help themselves first.

The woman unlimbered a lead pipe. There were bloodstains almost to the handle she'd made out of duct tape. I won't lie, I was nervous. My encounters with other survivors had been hit or miss, from the nice folks at the RV park to the army led by McQuinn. I was about as trusting as a rat guarding the last piece of moldy cheddar on earth.

The man lifted his jacket and showed a pair of revolvers. He didn't make any other moves.

"Well shit, I guess we're friends now," I shrugged, and followed Joel, hoping the man wouldn't shoot me in the back.

"I'm Tomas, and this is Doroyeta."

"Dori, like the fish from *Finding Nemo*," she said, and smiled.

"Creed, Jackson Creed. And that guy is Joel Kelly."

Movement at the door. The first Z came in and sized us up. He actually looked surprised, but that could be because his mouth was stuck wide open, thanks to a broken jaw. Tomas reached into his jacket, drew his gun, and calmly shot the monstrosity in the face. The Z went down but was soon replaced by two more. To make matters worse, I thought I'd heard a shuffler out there.

"Shit, man. Windows got bars. I guess we check the room with the locked door."

I rolled my eyes and prepared for the worst.

Survival of the Fastest

11:20 hours approximate
Location: Vista

I wanted to trust the couple, but it wasn't easy. This was a different world. Gone were the days of small talk, neighbors who helped each other out, and even passive-aggressive comments. What had become the norm--the social media-driven Facebook world--was toast, hell, the internet was deader than a zombie. Now it was down to survival of the fastest.

Joel listened at the door for a half second then muttered, "Fuck it."

He stepped back, lifted his foot, and smashed the door in. It splintered around the lock and flew open to crash against the wall. I fumbled for my wrench, fighting all of the gear and shit that was hanging from my pack. The strap caught in the stock of the little assault rifle, so I ripped it to the side, banging the stock against my elbow in the process.

The room was something out of a nightmare.

The wall was liberally smeared with blood. Equal amounts of red stained the bedspread where it lay in a heap at the foot of the bed. The sheets were also a mishmash of gore and blood and the carpet, light brown, was splotched with blood stains.

A picture hung on the wall, at an angle. It was the famous painting by Edvard Munch, called *The Scream*. Not that I was an art expert, but who didn't know this work? I also had owned a print of it when I was a kid. Mom thought it was something that would make me smile. It gave me nightmares for years, but I never had the heart to tell her.

The room contained a dresser with most of its drawers hanging open.

A pathetic looking Z lay on the ground. He'd been eaten almost to the bone around his abdomen, and most of a leg was gone. He lifted his head to look us over, then dropped it again, hitting the wall right next to the door. That explained the banging.

Another Z came at us. She'd been near the corner of the room, staring at nothing in particular. I didn't even see her at first, because she was garbed in a dark dress and standing next to even darker drapes. She tripped over the Z and fell, hands out, so she caught Joel and dragged him to the ground.

The couple moved in fast, taking her by the arms and hauling her off. The man pushed her against the wall and the woman bashed in her forehead with the lead pipe. She fell in a heap and her head lolled to the side. Sightless white eyes regarded me.

Dori then took mercy on the man on the floor, two strong blows leaving a pile of rotted brains.

I grasped Joel's hand and helped him up.

Joel moved toward the back of the room and peeked inside a door.

"Bathroom's empty," he said.

The door banged at the front of the house.

"Any way out?" I asked Joel as he eyed the bathroom.

He shook his head.

"Guess that means we're going to have company," I said. "We need to get the hell out of dodge, partner."

"Check the window," Joel said.

I moved the drapes aside.

Something crashed inside the house, rattling the walls. Moans and snarls came from the hallway.

"Bars!" I yelled for Joel. He joined me at the window but didn't say a word.

"Now what?" I shrugged.

The couple pushed the door shut but it wouldn't stay closed, because my Marine pal had destroyed the doorknob with his big Marine foot. Brilliant, Joel.

"This isn't good," he said.

###

He looked around the room for some egress point. He didn't need me to tell him that there wasn't one.

I unlatched the window and it slid open with a squeal. Joel joined me, and together we tested the bars. They had been constructed on a row so that they were welded together and set into the opening. Joel grabbed the windowsill and put his foot on the jamb. He tested the bars with a quick outward kick.

The couple grabbed the corners of a large dresser and grunted as they slid it across the floor toward the door.

"Wanna know how I know we're fucked?" I asked Joel.

"How?"

"Because that shit never works in the movies," I nodded toward the door-damming operation.

Joel snorted and kicked the bars again.

My pack was in the way so I shrugged it off and then fought all of the extra gear into a pile. My wrench stayed across my back.

I moved beside Joel and lifted my leg, hoping that my recently-healed sprain wasn't going to be a problem.

"On three," Joel said.

I nodded.

He counted and together we kicked the poles. It was like kicking a brick wall.

"Again," he said.

Again we got the same reaction.

"Watch out, Joel." I ripped the wrench off my shoulder and maneuvered it between a pair of bars.

Joel took this cue and moved aside. He grabbed the little home invasion rifle we'd dug up in the other room and examined it. He fiddled with a switch on the side, checked the magazine, inspected the trigger assembly, and then moved away to help the couple.

He dropped a box of shells on the ground, and with deft and well-practiced fingers, loaded the magazine.

"We can't hold for long," Tomas said.

"Got it," I replied.

I pulled the wrench and got a little give from the bars.

The Zs smashed against the door. I looked over my shoulder and caught the entrance budging. Joel motioned for the couple to move out of the way. He lifted the little SIG, aimed, and fired. Not for the first time, I wished I had some ear protection.

In the movies, the shots weren't this loud. Dudes shot each other and then had quiet conversation about drug dealers and the best way to break someone's knee. In this room, the gun might as well have been mortars going off around us.

The gun bucked under his arms, and something dropped on the other side of the doorway.

"I like this thing," Joel said.

I wedged the wrench a little tighter and pulled.

Christ, we did not have time for this!

Joel fired several more shots, but there was always an answer in the form of something banging against the entrance. The next time the door moved, a hand darted inside.

Dori pulled her knife and slammed it into the palm, pinning the Z to the doorway. Joel stuck the barrel of the gun into the gap and fired. When Dori yanked the knife free, the hand fell away from the doorframe, hopefully attached to a twice-dead fuck.

Tomas pushed her out of the way and pulled his guns. Dori fell back and shot him a dirty look. A smattering of a language I didn't understand ensued. He snarled an answer back at her. She turned away in disgust and moved to my side.

"I can help?" she said.

"I don't think so," I said, and jammed the wrench between a pair of bars.

Joel shot something. Tomas shot something. I wanted to look, but forced my attention to stay on the task at hand.

"Open the mouth," Dori looked up at me from under dark curls.

"Huh?"

"I show you," she said.

Dori took the wrench from me and gently pushed into the spot I'd occupied, shooing me out of the way. She propped the head against the window jamb and then loosened the teeth so the span opened a few inches.

"Help me. We put on bar, there, and we have leverage."

"Jesus," I said, suddenly seeing it.

"Jesus isn't here, only the dead," she said.

With the teeth of the wrench stuck against the wall and the other part against the bar, I suddenly had something to work with. I grabbed the handle up high so I would get the most control, and yanked, putting my body into it.

The bar popped off and the bolt hit the ground. I quickly worked at the next bar. One down, and too many more to go.

Joel fired off a few more rounds.

"How we looking?" I called.

"The bodies are making a nice blockade out there. Door's still not gonna hold," Joel called back.

Several somethings hit the door hard enough to rattle the dresser. Then they hit it again.

Joel took a step back and unleashed half a dozen shots at the door. The ensuing thump of a form hitting the ground answered.

I popped off the third bar and found the fourth to be a mother. Dori and I both worked at it for a minute, but it wasn't moving. She guided me to another one. It came off with a nice groan, leaving just two more bars.

Something pushed into the door again.

Hands reached for Tomas.

The window led to a backyard that was butted up against an apartment building. There was a small chainlink fence that ran the perimeter but several sections had collapsed, while others sagged. A few Zs roamed the yard, but nothing we couldn't deal with. The trick, as always, was to take them out quietly. Cave in a few heads and avoid attracting a horde.

Another Z had managed to weasel its way inside the room.

Joel fired until the gun was empty, and set it down.

"Where'd you put those .40 rounds?" he asked me.

I wiped a line of sweat off my forehead and nodded toward my backpack. Joel unzipped the bag and dug around, pulling out boxes of ammo.

The door rattled again and this time, the dresser was partially bucked into the room. Tomas shot something in the face, but another Z was right there to take its place.

The last bar wasn't budging. I was pretty sure Dori would be able to squeeze out of the room and maybe Joel Kelly, too, but I was stuck. Tomas was portly, so he wasn't going, either. Maybe we could shoot out the wall and crash through. Maybe we could slither up into the ceiling after bashing a hole with my wrench.

Both options were pretty far-fetched. With my luck I'd get halfway into the ceiling only to be dragged back into the room while a pair of Zs ate my legs.

Dori looked over her shoulder, fear etched upon her face. She pressed the wrench head onto the last bar, but up high this time.

Joel had a few boxes on the ground and he was going through them, but a whole lot of cursing accompanied his actions.

"I'll hold. You kick," Dori said.

"What if I break your wrist or hand?"

"Take risk or we die," she nodded toward the door.

"Fuck it," I muttered.

"Exactly. Fuck it," she said.

Dori held the wrench low on the grip and then dropped down as far as she could. I lifted my leg and braced myself on the window frame. I put my foot up and pressed against the wrench. If I didn't get this right, she'd have some broken digits.

I pulled my foot back and then kicked the wrench handle, but I was so concerned about her hand that I barely tapped it.

The dresser got pushed halfway into the room; a pair of very determined and very freshly turned Zs pushed on the door until it gave.

Joel stumbled back, managed to load his handgun, snapped the magazine home, lifted, aimed, and blew one of the bastards' heads off. The guy had been dressed in a sky-blue running suit complete with a bright green headband. He had a mullet that didn't look any better covered in gore.

The second Z was just as fast and dressed in the same gear, but in a ridiculous orange.

What a pair of assholes.

It got ahold of Tomas and dragged him to the ground. There was a brief struggle, but Tomas was strong and didn't put up with any of the Z's crap. He knocked the guy to the side and then rolled over. He was on his feet with a snarl. The Z grabbed Tomas's leg and tried to get a piece. Tomas ripped free and kicked the dead guy in the face. I was really starting to like this scrappy fighter.

The Z fell away but Tomas wasn't done. He rolled over and drove his knife into the Z's face, yanked it out, and did it again.

The dresser moved again, and more Zs barged into the room.

I kicked the wrench again and the bar budged.

"Come on," Dori urged me on.

I pulled my boot back and slammed it into the wrench, catching the edge of Dori's finger. She didn't have time to pull back, because the bar snapped free.

"Out!" I yelled.

Tomas came to his feet and kicked another Z. It fell back into the crowd at the door, creating a temporary roadblock. Joel fired a pair of shots and then came at us. I moved aside, but he urged me to go ahead.

I helped Dori out the window and Tomas was right behind her.

Joel shot a pair of Zs while he jammed stuff back into my backpack. Boxes of rounds and empty magazines were stuffed in. He tried to zip it closed but I reached over, grabbed it, and tossed it out the window.

"Dude, let's go!"

Joel grinned, rose to his feet, and calmly shot a female Z in the forehead. She'd been covered in blood, her hair like some kind of nightmare of bright red dreads. She went down and then Joel was tossing our shit outside.

"Piece of cake," he said, and then lifted his foot and shrugged out the window like he was about to go for a leisurely Sunday walk around the city.

I was right behind him. A Z managed to grab hold of my shirt but I shook his hand off. When I was outside I picked up my wrench and crushed the Z's head that came at us. The next one crowded in, so I bashed it just as hard. The two bodies created a nice little dam that would buy us some time.

"Piece of cake, my ass," I muttered.

I grabbed my bag, shifted stuff around until it would close, and then worked it around my shoulders.

Dori and Tomas had advanced into the yard and taken out a pair of Zs, nice and quietly. He got a young guy's attention and backed away, and she shattered in the back of the Z's head. The last one was a guy who had to be in his seventies and weigh close to three hundred pounds. Tomas tripped him and Dori smashed his head to pulp. They nodded at each other and then turned to regard us.

"I like them. They're the model of killing efficiency we should all strive for," Joel said like a typical Marine.

"I like them too, because they're alive and they're not trying to kill us," I muttered back.

11:25 hours approximate
Location: Vista

The lawn was just as dead as our pursuers. Adobe had been set in a sidewalk of sorts and then outlined in fist-sized stones. Plants wilted in pots, except for three palm trees. They rose three or four feet and didn't look any worse for wear. A few more years and the owners had probably planned to plant them around the perimeter of the house. One thing that southern California didn't lack for was palm trees.

Someone had posted a sign: "Don't be a dope. Clean up your dog's poop." Someone else had scrawled "Brains" over the word "poop".

A pair of legs lay, unmoving from beneath some shrubs. I didn't bother investigating, because--zombies.

We'd only been in the house for fifteen or twenty minutes, but the sky had turned a nasty shade of grey. San Diego didn't really have a winter--it was seventy year-round--but this November had become dismal in the early weeks. I was convinced it was because the world currently sucked ass. More than likely, it was just a normal weather pattern. If rain broke out right now I'd be happy. That meant precipitation would pool up so we wouldn't have to rely on bottled water for the rest of our (presumably) short lives.

Joel motioned for us to drop. The Hungarians caught on and went into a crouch. We shuffled low until we were behind a planter box. A small horde of ten or fifteen dead meandered past our position. A straggler took an interest in the fence because Zs are stupid, and decided to hang out for a while.

Tomas pulled a gun, but Joel shook his head.

I snapped my fingers to get the Z's attention. It lifted its head and drooled blood.

The kid couldn't have been more than fifteen years old, and that made me think of Craig.

The Z didn't catch on, so I snapped my fingers again.

He walked into the fence and then fell over. His ass was in the air and his hands were on the ground. I maneuvered around the planter, wrench in a tight grip.

Something caught my eye at the corner of the yard where the fence met the back of the house. A shape came into view and then faded again.

I waited, hand lifted slightly to tell Joel to wait. When I didn't see the form again, I advanced on the kid.

He was dressed in the remains of a pair of tighty-whiteys. The only other thing that he wore was one red knee-length sock. His back and arms were a mess of wounds that were hard to look at. No one, especially not a kid, should have to go through that kind of trauma.

"What are you waiting for?" Joel hissed.

I stared at the kid. He was stuck, and his legs were kicking in slow motion. His hands scrabbled at the ground, but as much as he wanted to crawl toward me, he didn't have the motor skills to pull himself off the fence.

Thing about killing Zs is you get used to it. Sure, I've seen my share of the dead wanting to take a bite. I'd fought back, because that was survival. What I hated was all the necessary killing. This was no different.

11:50 hours approximate
Location: Vista

"Where to, boss?" the Hungarian man asked.

"Tomas. I don't want to be rude but we don't exactly have room for more people in our little group."

"We help, then we and you go."

"Why?"

Tomas stared at me like I was an idiot.

"It is normal to help, yes?" Dori chimed in.

"Fine. Ya'll wanna help, that's great, but we're

not far from our base of operations. When we get back, we're out of this city," Joel said.

He was being purposefully obtuse. No sense revealing too much to folks we didn't know. It was like I had a psychic connection to my pal. Neither one of us had found a reason to trust another human, but I wasn't going to turn them away if they were going to help with my plan. The plan I hadn't told Joel about yet.

We hid behind the burned-out husk of a doublewide that had probably been a piece of shit even before it had been set on fire. The roof was bent the wrong way and hung inside the monstrosity, judging by the limited view I got from the kicked-in doorway. I was pretty sure one of the blackened husks on the floor had been a person.

The house next to the doublewide backed up to a sprawling trailer park that was littered with debris and bodies. One of the homes was at least intact, but something thumped against the walls and wasn't being quiet about it.

I motioned for Joel to join me, and we moved a few feet away.

"No, man. We can't bring them," Joel said before I could get a word in.

"I know that. I need to do something and I understand if you want to get back to our base."

"Stupid sailor. What half-assed plan are you about to get killed over?"

"So little faith, Joel. Have I steered us wrong

yet?"

"Yeah. Many times."

I gave Joel a flat look.

"Alright. What is it? We can't keep tossing houses all day."

"I know, but I have to come back with antibiotics. Anna's wound can't wait."

Tomas and Dori kept watch. He spoke to her in Hungarian and she nodded. Both of them took pains to pretend like they weren't listening to us.

"Even if we found a pharmacy, place has probably been picked over twenty times."

"Remember the piece of paper?" I said, and lowered my backpack.

I moved aside cans, boxes of ammo and boxed food until I found the sheet and pulled it out. One side had been a poster for a rock band from the eighties. The other held the message.

"Probably a trap," he said and handed it back.

"So we scout it out and get our new friends here to help."

"What's in it for them?"

"Maybe they have needs that can be met."

I motioned for Dori and Tomas to join us, and told them what I had in mind.

A shambler moved past the burned-out house, but didn't catch wind of us. We kept silent for a few minutes while its mindless legs carried it away from our position.

"We have needs too. We go," Tomas said.

Dori said something in Hungarian and he

shook his head. They spoke together, her sounding pissed, him sounding like he didn't care.

"I apologize. We must leave you now," Dori waved her hand, indicating our location. "After we are clear of this place we go."

Tomas didn't look happy, but he nodded.

"It's cool, I understand," I said. "Maybe we'll run into each other again."

They probably didn't trust us either, but at least they were being civil and not trying to shoot us in the back and take our stuff. The only reason we'd joined up in the first place was because we didn't have a choice.

We nodded at each other and together moved out. Joel and I scouted, while they followed and covered our backs. The two were smart and keep their eyes up and focused. They worked well as a team; I couldn't help but think about the value of adding them to our little group of misfits.

We made good time as we ducked into homes and buildings, constantly on the lookout for Zs. As much as I'd come to expect threats around every corner, under every car, inside every doorway, we only came across a few, and they went down quickly and best of all, quietly.

As we neared the center of town, I broke out the little map again and looked at street signs and landmarks.

Dori and Tomas made short farewells, and then they moved out. A minute later and they hunkered down between two homes, then ran to a road and stayed near a low line of shrubs.

"Shame they couldn't stick around," Joel said. "The little firecracker was growing on me."

"Me too," I nodded. "But I don't think any of us were ready to shake hands and become BFFs. Plus, how do we feed two new mouths? It's hard enough to keep *ourselves* fed, not to mention the shit machine known as Frosty."

"Maybe we'll get lucky and come across an overturned tortilla chip truck. I'd just about kill for a bag of Doritos."

"You had to mention chips. One of the greatest inventions in the world and we can't find a snack-size bag to save our lives."

I thought I was going to start drooling. Hell, I'd take a shower in Doritos and call it the perfect day.

12:15 hours approximate
Location: Vista

The map had been crude but well done. A simple sketch work of lines representing streets as well as one landmark: that being a street roundabout that contained a fountain that was dry as a desert. There was a statue of some guy on top, and tied to him were the corpses of two of Zs who'd been executed. Their rotting husks hung over the fountain and had given it a rust color, thanks to all the blood. Whoever had shot these two hadn't been kind. Bullet holes riddled every body part.

A dog ran across the street, barking at the top of his lungs, but was gone before I could think to quiet him down.

We found the convenience store we'd raided an hour ago and then studied the street signs again. I pointed at one labeled La Jolla and Joel nodded. The street was free of bodies, but cars had been pushed into an interesting pattern. Joel and I hunkered behind one while we studied the lay of the land.

"This shit is creepy."

"What do you mean?" I asked.

"It's been done up to slow us down."

"Or slow down Zs," I said.

Joel's assault rifle was pressed against his shoulder. He stared into the EOTech scope.

"Could be. Could be a trap."

"Agreed, but why a trap if they want to barter?"

"Shoot the folks coming in the gauntlet and take their shit. Drag the bodies off somewhere," Joel said.

I gulped.

"How about this. I'll go ahead in and you cover me."

"No shit, Sherlock. Think we're both gonna just wander into a death trap?" he said.

"Wouldn't be the first time," I said, and stood up.

"Keep your head down. If anyone starts

shooting, I'll shoot back."

"I know, man. Just don't shoot me in the ass."

Joel nodded and I moved out.

###

12:30 hours approximate
Location: Vista

I felt like I was under the crosshairs the entire time. The gauntlet, as Joel had called it, was just that: trucks, cars, furniture--anything that could be used as an obstacle--had been dragged into the street to form a maze. Spikes made out of sticks and metal tubing had been driven into the sides of vehicles to catch unwary Zs. Bodies hung from some traps, but they were fresh kills.

I didn't see anything resembling a freshly-killed human. Only rotted flesh, bald and balding heads, and a whole lot of blood and rot. Pretty typical stuff for the apocalypse.

I glanced back, expecting to see Joel, but I should have known better. He'd disappeared, however I didn't think for a minute that he'd abandoned me. Like a Marine hedgehog, he'd probably found some place to get nice and invisible and had the area I was waltzing into under his sights.

I didn't want to think about the alternative, that someone had him and me under *their* sights, especially since I was probably walking into a trap.

What I wouldn't give to have some kind of

Bluetooth radio headset to talk to Joel as I walked toward my death.

But I had to do this for Anna. I needed to get her antibiotics, or the bullet extraction could go south real quick like. Assuming Roz could even get the damn bullet out, having Frosty lick the wound probably wouldn't do much good. I needed to get her the drugs Roz had listed.

I came across a crudely-drawn sign done up with a Sharpie.

"No ZEDs within. Advance to safety, state what you have to barter, then get the fuck out. Wrong move gets you erased."

What was the wrong move exactly? Was I supposed to leave my weapons here?

"Leave your weapons and come on in," a voice called from the shadow. Damn, that guy should have been on psychic hotline.

I dropped to a crouch and ducked next to a burned-out sedan. My wrench was in one hand and my pistol was in the other.

"If we wanted you dead we'd a shot you a while back. You're a big fella," a husky female voice said.

"I haven't exactly had the best luck with other people," I said lamely.

"I know. We're not animals. Just here to trade and get you back on the road to wherever the hell you're going. Oh, and we're not Reavers, because fuck those guys."

"Reavers?" I asked.

"Those wackos that want to see the world burn. We're businessmen, not bullies."

I shook my head. Reavers?

"I don't know anything about assholes burning the world. How about if I just turn around and go back the way I came right now?" I asked.

"Have a nice day, but feel free to come back when you need something. We got a whole shop fulla goods. Just ask. We probably got it. See ya," she said.

"Fuck," I whispered.

"Not my type," she said.

"So you're not going to steal my stuff?"

"Hell no. We need guys like you to bring back goodies. For the love of Pete, show yourself, Devon."

A person materialized a few feet from me. He'd been hiding in a dark doorway, and he was dressed all in black, including a ski mask. I guessed that he was one of the figures that had nodded at me earlier in the day. He had a sidearm, holstered, and some kind of assault rifle I'd never seen before but Joel could probably write a love poem about.

Anna needed this.

I put my pistol aside and dropped my wrench.

"Fine. I'm leaving my pistol and wrench here. I have backup, though, so don't do anything stupid."

"Black fella with a hard face? Yeah, we know about him. Just play it cool and no one gets holey.

That's what happens when bullets start to fly. People drop to the ground and start praying to god. Plus there's the actual holes. Nasty business."

I lifted my hands and moved around the car. There was a low wooden door, and behind that stood a woman in her fifties or sixties. She was whip-thin and had a crazy mop of curly white hair. Thick glasses rode her nose. She smiled, though, and I wondered if I was going to take that as my last sight before I woke up in hell.

"You *are* a big one. Just keep a calm head and we'll do the same. Got guys coming and going all the time, but it's always the first-timers that are twitchy. We've been in business for a week and only one person's messed this up. He's out there, on the side of a car. Keeps the Zs away," she cackled.

"So how does this work?" I asked and lowered my hands. I tried to eye the man in black but he'd disappeared. Instead I lifted my hand in the air and did a little circle so Joel knew I wasn't in immediate danger.

"How do ya *think* it works? Ya come in here, tell me what ya need, and I tell you what *I* need. If we got stuff to trade then we smile, give each other our stuff, and part friends. Handshakes are optional."

"What if I don't have what you need?"

"I bet you could make an old woman feel good," she smiled and winked at me.

"Thought I wasn't your type," I said and

thought about just leaving.

"Mom, leave him alone," a voice called from inside.

The woman broke into another cackle and gestured for me to join her.

"I'm just messing with ya. Name's Elda. Come on in, we got some hot beef stew. Ain't the best, 'cause it's from a can, but it's warm and fills ya up. Guy came in needing some bandages and left us a case. I'll share if it makes ya feel any better. You can even watch me sip it if it makes ya feel safer."

I was practically drooling at the mention of stew.

"Fine. Just make it quick if you're going to kill me," I muttered. "I don't want to die knowing I let my friends down."

"So melodramatic. Just barter and then go along your way. I won't hold it against ya if ya don't want stew or hospitality."

I considered the older woman. This might be an act. A really good act. A few weeks ago I probably would have trusted her. After McQuinn I wasn't in the mood to trust anyone. But I did my best to keep my wits about me.

She opened the wooden door and gestured, then turned and kept talking as she walked. I followed, wary of anyone that might jump out and try to plant a knife in my skull.

"We have some food, ammo, and meds. Most people want meds, but we're fresh out of Oxy. I guess the next best thing would be to go to L.A.

and find someone that deals heroin, then stick a needle up your ass and say goodbye to this shitty world for a few hours."

"How's L.A.?" I couldn't help but ask.

"Still there, last I heard, but ya have to watch out for the Reavers. The city took a lot of damage, but I heard some mercenaries working with the military have cleared up part of the city and they're fighting the Reavers. There's talk of big walls, but I don't know--could just be talk. If you're heading up there I suggest you approach by daylight. Also heard they shoot anything that creeps around at night."

"That's the second time I've heard the term Reavers. Who are they?"

"You *are* wet behind the ears," she said with a half-smile. "We don't know much, but when they appear we disappear. They're some kind of wackos who think God brought on this plague and it's their job to convince unbelievers with fire or bullets. Rumor has it they took over some military bases or they were already *on* bases, inside job and such, can't say for sure. They're bad news. Look for the bloody skullcaps."

"Bloody skullcaps? The hell is wrong with people?" I shook my head.

"People got guns now and no one to tell 'em to put 'em away. All that shootin'. Figure they'd run out of ammo at some point. Then I guess stuff will get medieval. Swords and maces. Like that big ole wrench you carry. I heard about you from my boy

Devon, out front."

I nodded as she kept talking.

"You just steer clear of Reaver camps, you'll be okay. Not sure I'd recommend going to L.A., but it's your skin. Now, what do ya need?"

She'd taken over an antique store. Old clothes and collectibles had been piled on shelves and counters. A typewriter that had seen better days fifty years ago sat in a corner with a fresh sheet of paper protruding from the roller. Plates, picture frames, and a chair that had a spin seat and a weird thick wicker back were all pushed aside. Boxes of MREs, bottled water, and cases of soup and vegetables were stacked in one corner.

"Antibiotics."

"Oh yeah? Someone sick?"

"Something like that. What do you have?"

"What do you need?"

I reached into my pocket and found the crumpled-up note that Roz had prepared. I tried to pronounce the first pill on the list, but after I'd butchered it for the second time, Elda grabbed the slip of paper.

"I got one of these. I think. I'll have to have my son take a look."

Someone slipped out of a corner of the room. He was dressed in the same shade of "don't fuck with me" black as the guy near the doorway outside. He wore a couple of guns, but one was under his arm and his right hand stayed close to the stock. This did nothing to make me feel safe.

"Hi," I said lamely.

"Yo," the guy nodded.

He took the list and disappeared into the back of the store. A lock clicked and he rummaged around.

"I don't have much. Some canned goods, a box of crackers. Half a can of Easy Cheese. Got a burner and some butane," I said, and hefted my bag.

"Not bad."

The guy returned with a couple of pill bottles and handed them to the woman. She squinted at the labels.

"I have ten Amoxicillin That's good for a few days. What kind of wound are we talking about?"

"Gunshot," I said, and didn't elaborate.

The itching feeling on the back of my neck, like someone had a gun pointed at my head, wouldn't depart.

"Let me see the burner."

I lowered my pack with a clank. The burner was stuffed in the top so that it barely closed. I had three bottles of fuel, which I also set out. The thing was, this was something we could really use, but Anna needed the meds. If she got infected there was no way to take her to a hospital or clinic. An infection could easily become a death sentence.

"I'll let ya have five pills for the burner and butane."

"Come on," I protested. "I need those pills."

"You and folks with a lot more to offer. What

else ya got?"

I rolled my eyes and dug around in my bag, pushing aside the Percocets, TUMS, and the stuff I couldn't pronounce, until I found the last bottle of pills. I held them up to the light, and read the label out loud.

"Well, hell. Why didn't ya say so? Lotta folks living on antidepressants now that the end of the world is here. Kinda ironic, don't you think? Everyone felt like their world was ending and took pills. Now the world *is* over and they really *need* the goddamn pills."

"So you want these?" I stared into the bottle and figured there were at least fifty.

"Oh yeah. Take the antibiotics."

"Works for me," I said, and started to stuff the burner back into my backpack.

"And the burner?"

"I don't think so. See I'm a Navy hole snipe and that means I'm not all that bright. But I can count, and fifty of my pills are worth a hell of a lot more than ten of your pills. All things being equal and all."

The woman's son choked back a chuckle from his vantage point.

"I can throw in a few more pills."

"Sounds like a winner. Toss in a case of that beef stew while you're at it and we're good. Oh, and you have any 5.56 ammo?"

"Half case and two boxes of shells," she said.

I tossed her the pill bottle.

#

13:00 hours approximate
Location: Vista

"Are you fucking nuts, man? How are we going to hike back to the RV with our packs and that big-ass box?"

"I'm going to carry it, Joel, and you're going to shoot anything that looks at me in the wrong tone of voice," I said. "It's a case of beef stew. We're eating like kings tonight."

The box wasn't that heavy, but with my pack, weapons, wrench, and the case of food, it was going to be a long walk.

"You kidding me? You get the drugs?"

"Yeah and I got some interesting news. There's some fringe group called Reavers operating near L.A. The store owner told me they're a bunch of idiots in bloody skullcaps and they have an agenda that involves guns and fire."

"Wait, what?" Joel asked.

"That's all I know, man. We can't worry about it now, I guess. California's a big place and hopefully we won't run into them."

"We'll steer clear, and good fucking deal on the supplies, brother," he said. "We're a day out from Pendleton, and if I know my brothers they won't put up with this Reaver bullshit. We'll be safe once we get to the base."

I grinned at Joel and hefted the pack. He

moved out and I followed close behind.

I wish I could say that the Marine base was the start of our salvation. Turned out, we had a long way to go.

A Pair of Extractions

13:15 hours approximate
Location: Vista

The trek back to the RV was just as wretched as you can imagine. We ran, ducked, hid, shot, and bludgeoned stuff. We took out enough Zs to fill a small classroom, and then we did it again. There comes a point when the bodies fall away and you just have to wonder if they will ever end.

Joel kept looking back over his shoulder.

"What are you expecting?" I asked.

"Just don't trust the dealers. Wanna make sure they aren't following us."

I hadn't even thought of that, so paranoia crept into me and soon I was looking over my shoulder before every turn. Thankfully the men dressed in black didn't make a reappearance.

A Z was, though. He came out of a doorway and made for me.

I had no choice but to back away and carefully set the case of beef stew on the ground. In the time it took me to stand up, lift the wrench, and swing, I also had time to miss. The bastard hit a curb and stumbled so I hit air. Joel was already moving down the alley, so he didn't know I was in trouble. I hissed and called his name, but he didn't hear me, or maybe he was sick of saving my dumb ass and decided to leave me behind.

The Z was all rotting breath, yellow, and bloodstained teeth. One side of his head was torn away leaving muscle, sinew, and crusted blood. His other ear dangled by a strip of skin and flapped against the side of his head.

I pulled back but the Z was fresh, in that "I just got bit a few days ago and most of my limbs still work" kinda way that was real damn annoying.

I used one of my best weapons, my foot, and pushed the fool back. He grabbed my ankle and leaned over to bite me, so I swung the wrench again and connected with his shoulder. He took the blow and almost went down, but his grip on my ankle pulled me off-balance and I stumbled, striking my knee on the curb. Pain shot up my thigh, so hot and sharp I had to fight back a scream.

The dead fuck fell away as I managed to sit back on my ass and shake him lose. I rolled to the side and got a fresh shambler around my neck for the effort. Jesus Christ! Were they *breeding* back there?

I did the only thing I could think of: I lowered my chin to my chest and then snapped my head back hard, catching the Z right in the face. Cartilage broke and something cold and wet hit my neck. Fighting back nausea and an intense wish to find all of the Purell in the world to squirt down my shirt, I stood up, dragging the Z along with me.

It dropped in a pile of arms and legs, fighting to get to its feet. The first Z came at me, so I backed up a step, knee aching as it took my full weight. I shuddered but soldiered on.

"Joel," I called, but my voice was a ragged gasp.

The pair of Zs closed in on me from opposite sides, both eyeing my pale white flesh. They probably looked at me the same way I'd look at a rack of baby back ribs covered in BBQ sauce. The stupid thought invaded my mind and saliva actually shot into my mouth.

"Here, piggy," I said, and bashed the first Z in the head.

He went down in a lump, my wrench stuck in his head. I had to let go or be dragged down to the ground, so that left me--with a full pack and assorted weapons clanking around my body--to stumble away as the zombie closed in.

She was about my age, and her wounds weren't as bad as those of the guy who had my weapon sticking out of his noggin. She was small but wiry, and fast. She moaned: that low rumble of greed for flesh that I'd heard endlessly since this shitstorm started.

I fell back and my leg went out from under me as pain made me grimace. One second I was on my feet, the next I was on my aching knees.

Her hair might have been a pale shade of red once, but now it was like knotted curtains around her head. When she spun around to track me, her dreads of gore spun with her, slapping against the side of her face. I never wanted to hear that noise again.

I managed to crawl a few feet, rip a can of beef stew off the pile and throw it at her. She took it in the chest, so I picked up another and pelted her in the neck. She snarled at me and staggered to her feet. Hands up, fingers mostly intact except for a few that were bent back at an angle that made me shudder, she crawled on her knees.

I smacked her with another can, but it hit her shoulder and the can sailed away.

I struggled to my feet, but the Z tripped on her shoelace and fell on me, taking me to the ground. I fought her as she went for my arms. She got a piece of fabric and ripped it in her greedy mouth. I punched her in the side of the head, feeling like a misogynistic asshole, and then hit her again. By the time I pounded her to the side I'd gotten over myself, stood up, and crushed her head.

Before I could breathe a sigh of relief, a fresh pair of Zs exited the building and stumbled toward me. I tried to get up, but my leg screamed in pain. It was the same leg I'd injured a few weeks ago, so my freshly-healed ankle now had company. That was just great.

"Fuck every one of you!" I said, realizing that I

was about to join their ranks.

Joel's knife blurred out and took one of the Zs in the temple. He was like some ninja as he let go of the blade and then lashed out a foot to trip the other Z.

"You gonna sit there crying or help me out?"

"I got a choice?" I said.

My wrench was only a few feet away. I shuffled toward it and grabbed the haft. The weapon felt good, like an extended arm terminating in a fist of heavy metal. I lifted the piece and then spun as one of the zombies broke from the cover of the building.

I struck it at about knee height, a staggering blow that took its legs out. The Z wasn't even on the ground when I hit it in the head a couple of times.

Joel helped me to my feet.

"Wondered where you were, then come to find out you're back here playing with some new friends."

"Fuckers came out of nowhere, man. There was one and then two. After that I lost count."

"That's because they don't teach squids how to count. You good?"

I put my arm around him and tested my weight on my leg. It ached but took the pressure, so I took a half step away.

"Jesus. Look at this mess. Let's haul ass before more of them come out of that clown car of a building and try to finish us off."

Joel chuckled.

"Gather up the cans and let's hit it." Joel grabbed one of the precious cylinders of stew and put it back on the box.

I grabbed two more and dropped them onto the crate, trying to ignore the blood and gore that were pasted to the sides of the cans. Where'd the last one go?

A pair of snarls made me forget about it. I grabbed the box, shouldered it, and staggered after Joel.

We moved around the block, ducked around some wilting hedges, and then stood and ran for it. Well, to be fair, Joel ran; I limped after.

Moans followed us.

After a pair of turns, we reached the block where we'd left the RV, came around the corner, and both stopped in our tracks.

The RV was gone.

But that wasn't the worst part. Sniffing around the ground the RV had occupied was a shuffler, and he was surrounded by a half dozen fresh Zs.

#

13:40 hours approximate
Location: Vista

The building had been a junkyard, and the Zs were prowling around rusting hulks of cars and car parts. One of the bastards had taken an interest in a bumper and kept nudging it with his foot.

That's not a person, you dumbass zombie.

We faded back behind the building. I held my breath and waited for the telltale sound of a shuffler's cry. If he'd spotted us we were going to have to either stand and fight--something I didn't relish--or run, something I wasn't going to be so good at.

Joel didn't say a word. He carefully lowered his pack and weapons. He leaned them against the house and gestured for me to do the same. I tried to keep the noise down and wasn't sure if I did a good job. The cans were first, then I had to maneuver a few of the weapons we'd snagged from the house onto the ground. My wrench was next, followed by my pack.

Joel touched my shoulder and motioned me close.

"The fuck we gonna do now?" I whispered next to his ear.

"It's gonna go down like the old days. You sneak around the back. I'll shoot a few, starting with that shuffler, in sixty seconds."

"Why the hell are we going to take on this bunch? Let's haul ass and regroup."

"There's a piece of paper taped to the side of the building. I think they left us a message. The girls wouldn't desert us unless they felt threatened. I think they left behind a clue."

"A clue? Been watching too much *CSI*?"

"I ain't seen a TV in months, ya dumbass," Joel said.

I rolled my eyes.

"So I'm bait and you're going to shoot them with what?"

"I have a few rounds for the AR. I can take out the shuffler, but after that it's going to get tough. You go in swinging and shooting once the shuffler's down."

"What if you miss?"

"When have I missed?"

"I don't know, about fifty times, give or take."

It was Joel's turn to roll his eyes.

"Fine. We go in shooting, we get eaten, should we leave a note while the shuffler's eating our brains?" Joel said.

"Our only other choice is to hide this stuff and then split up. We could each take a direction and try to find the RV. I'm betting they didn't go far."

A shot echoed to the east.

I looked at Joel, but he only shrugged.

"What, can't tell what kind of weapon from the sound? Could that be Anna's piece?"

"Man, I don't know what the fuck a gun sounds like unless it's an AK-47. Those things are distinct."

"It's like we speak two different languages, Joel. Okay, so the plan is like this: I flank 'em, go in swinging and shooting, and you kill the shuffler. It *is* like the old days."

The first week we'd been in San Diego, we'd become a tight fighting machine. Short, fast engagements resulting in twice-dead corpses, then we got scarce real fast, and hopefully with a few supplies for the effort. Things had changed as the shufflers had gotten smarter. I was also banged up pretty badly, and didn't even know if I'd be able to get around the building in time.

"We got this, man. It's going to be smooth as melted butter."

"Famous last words," I said, and looked at my watch.

"Sixty seconds," Joel said, and picked up his assault rifle. He looked it over, and then popped into a squat.

"Better make it seventy. I'm a mess."

"Getting slow in your old age?"

"No, man. Ankle's hurting like hell, shoulder's banged up, the feeling just came back to my knee and it's not a good kind of feeling."

"I'll give you a minute and a half to flank 'em. When I drop the shuffler, you go in swinging."

I dragged my pack to us and quietly unzipped it, then rummaged around inside for a few seconds.

Joel looked at me questioningly.

I found the small box of shells I'd picked up from the old woman and handed it to Joel. He smiled and slid the cover open.

"Merry early fucking Christmas," I said.

"Best gift ever," Joel said.

He popped the magazine out of his assault rifle and started loading it. I noticed there were only two rounds in the mag.

"Really, man? You were going to risk my life with two rounds."

"Gimme some credit. Two rounds equal two kills."

"Ninety seconds. You better not miss that damn shuffler."

Joel grunted, quietly slipped the full magazine back into the rifle and shot me a cool look. I nodded back, picked up my wrench and handgun, and moved out.

13:50 hours approximate
Location: Vista

I started this journal a few months ago. The first entry was about a mission just like this one. We were in the process of finding supplies for "fortress," and that meant making runs into town. As we ranged farther and farther out, we ran into problems with Zs as they got hungrier. I took to calling it "The Fuckening".

I was ultra-cautious back then and took little risk, except for the day we had to get past a bunch of Zs, and one of the quick ones I later came to call shufflers. Since then, the shufflers had grown smarter and could, much to my horror, control a small army of their undead brothers. I didn't know how the mechanism for communicating with their little minions worked, and I really didn't care. All I wanted was to kill every shuffler I came across. I wanted to bash in heads and then take a minute to piss on their corpses.

Just like the first days, I was about to do something dumb. I was about to be bait.

The building had seen better days before the z-poc and was now what I'd call comfortably dilapidated. Some kind of vines clung to one side and sunlight shone through space where the walls had been kicked or just fallen in. Two windows faced out, but both were devoid of glass. If it came down to it, I guessed I could just *Die Hard* my way through a window and hide under a desk. The problem with that plan? I'm no Bruce Willis.

I ran into my first difficulty as soon as I tried to move to the backside of the building. A big fence was in the way. It was chain-link, sure, and it wasn't all that tall. But it was going to be noisy as hell. Plus there was a wreck parked right next to the fence, and there was no way I was risking tetanus today.

My internal clock was about to hit forty-five seconds, so I needed to move with a purpose.

I crept alongside the fence and found another building that was probably someone's house. The doors had been mostly boarded up, but a limp and half-devoured body lay near the remains of the wood planks that were scattered all over the busted-ass porch.

I skirted the building at a near sprint before rounding it and finding the path clear. Then it was just a matter of another thirty or so feet. I reached the edge of the building and peeked around. The Zs were still there, but the shuffler wasn't in sight. The fact that we had no way to communicate--like those cool little throat mics that the mercenaries had possessed when we were in the city of Vista--sucked.

There was no real plan, except that it was go time. My internal clock dinged at ninety seconds, so I strode out into the open.

The first Z saw me as soon as I saw it. I lifted the wrench in my right hand and pointed the gun with my left. Not that I was ever a good shot, and sure as shit not at all good with my off hand, but I had still learned a thing or two about shooting Zs.

"Hey, you godless fucks," I said.

Joel was not in sight, but I assumed he was low and at the corner of a building, covering me from a forty-five degree angle so I didn't accidentally shoot him.

The thing snarled at me. Three others turned their milky white gazes on me and staggered. I aimed, exhaled, and fired, expecting to miss the first time, because I'm sharp like that.

I fired and the Z took a round in the neck. It spun around and dropped to one knee.

The others didn't care about their buddy. They saw me and thought I was human steak.

A shot rang out, and one of them dropped.

Where the hell was that fucking shuffler?

I took a half-dozen steps, pulled the wrench back, and flattened the Z who was on his knees.

His head turned inside out, and that was okay with me. Pulped brain matter exploded and hit the ground. He dropped without another sound and lay on his new pillow of squished and gnarly rot.

A pair broke from cover and came at me. Another shot and one of them fell over. His head snapped to the side like he'd just remembered something. Most of his face was gone. What in the hell kind of bullets had the old woman traded to me?

A pile of car parts that could use a bath in WD-40 provided a decent amount of cover as I dropped to a crouch and took cover.

An old man in golf shorts and the remains of a tank top looked around in a daze. In general, I don't recommend playing peek-a-boo with the dead. He was dark-skinned from time in the sun, time he'd spent before the change hit. If zombies got sunburned, I kind of felt bad for them.

Kind of.

I switched hands and used my much better right to aim. The gun bucked and the Z fell on its face with a neat hole in the side of its head. Damn, I was having a good day. Three shots and two kills. That was some Joel Kelly heroics right there.

The last Z was slow because he was dragging the remains of his foot. His ripped and shattered ankle hit the ground with each step, making a grinding noise. I gulped and aimed.

That's when a fresh wave broke from cover and came at me. There weren't just a few--there were at least ten or fifteen, and they were spry.

They'd been in the small alleyway across from our position. The sun had provided cover, and I wished I had a grenade to toss at the horde, because I was sure that's where the damn shuffler was holding court.

Joel broke from cover and came in shooting. I didn't wait around for him to accidentally shoot me; I headed for the side of a building. With my back against wood, I picked a target and shot him. He didn't drop, but I'd scored a hit, judging by the way he spun away.

A series of loud retorts echoed as Kelly moved in. He wasn't wasting time on theatrics; he was all badass Marine. His weapon was up and his eyes glued to targets. He dropped three in rapid succession as he strode onto the battlefield.

I took aim and shot another one, scoring a blast to the face. She probably hadn't been much to look at before death, and now she sprouted a third eye. Her legs went out from under her as she collapsed.

Something blurred across the ground and was in the air before I could fire. Joel dropped his aim and shifted to the side as the shuffler landed. He lashed out with his foot, but the shuffler was already moving. I wanted to rush to help, but there was an army of Zs to deal with.

I did my best to keep my cool as four of the bastards closed in on me. They weren't fast, not by a long shot, and each sported wounds. One was missing most of an arm, so I automatically labeled him as less of a threat. I went for the fastest one first, shooting him in the head. The chamber slammed back, waiting for me to reload, but I didn't have a fresh mag, so I dropped the gun back in its holster.

Taking up a slugger's stance, I knocked down one of the Zs, but there were still two to contend with, and they were already on me.

Out of the corner of my eye I caught sight of Joel. He slammed the shuffler in the side of the head with the butt of his rifle and then spun, dropped low, and took another one in the gut. His motions were timed and well-delivered.

I pushed one back into the other and swung, but missed and hit his arm. The Z didn't react to the blow--something that would have made a normal man scream in pain. The second Z was faster than I'd anticipated and moved on me. She was middle-aged, with grey-streaked hair that stuck up from a short haircut and a bunch of hair products consisting of blood and zombie goo.

She hit me hard, pushing my much larger frame into the wall. I levered myself forward by kicking back with my good leg. She fell back, but her arms came up in the classic zombie pose.

Joel was surrounded and fighting for his life. The shuffler had backed away, but I could tell he was preparing to leap.

I didn't have time for dealing with this Z. Instead of fighting her, I spun her around, picked her up, and barreled through the other zombie.

The stinkbeast in my arms was so foul it made me want to projectile vomit for about an hour. Her arms were covered in wounds, and she leaked from pretty much everywhere.

The shuffler turned his rabid green eyes on me and snarled. I didn't give him a chance to leap, lifting the moaning zombie in my arms, and slamming into him.

He was skinny as a rail and his hair was long and lank. He'd been low to the ground, on all fours. The three of us rolled around--tussling, I guess you'd call it, although I also thought of it later as fighting for my life.

I drove my knee into the shuffler's stomach, but he was quick as a whip. His hands lashed out over and over, striking at me. I got my arms up to protect my face and batted his hands aside. The Z I'd used for a battering ram rolled over and struggled to get up.

I took a blow to the head, from the shuffler, but exchanged my protection for a strike. I threw from the shoulder, something I'd done many times, and smashed the shuffler in the face. His nose exploded from the blow and his head smashed into the ground. This gave me enough of a breather to strike him again, but he got his head to the side, so I only struck his ear.

The other Z managed to get to her feet and attack. Why she went after me when Joel was busy fighting off three Zs was weird. Was she holding a grudge, or was this stupid shuffler using some odd mental telepathy, or some kind of unspoken language?

Joel was surrounded, but went for his sidearm. He drew and fired and then clicked on empty. The Z he'd shot fell away but was still moving.

The woman I'd used as a battering ram got on her hands and feet and then lunged for me. I was bowled over, and away from the shuffler. I wasn't just mad that she hit me; I'd had the damn shuffler right under me, and a chance to kill him. Now he was free.

The breath rushed out of my body as I struck the ground. I tried to roll into it, but with my legs busted up it was a shock I wasn't knocked flat.

The Z grabbed me, so I grabbed her back and pushed her down. The shuffler hit me hard enough to make my head spin, and then leapt.

Joel backed up and tugged his knife. Jesus Christ! We were getting our asses kicked here.

I was just about out of gas. I managed to hold of the Z, but she was strong and managed to trip me up. She fell on me and her mouth snapped next to my exposed neck. I pushed her head away, but she leaned in and almost got part of my cheek.

Joel managed to slash the shuffler, but the other zombies were closing in on both of us. The largest tripped on part of a carburetor and almost bowled Joel over. He grabbed Joel's boot and tried to bite him.

I ripped my eyes away from Joel when a gunshot cracked. The Z on top of me slumped to the side. Her blood, cold and thick, hit my face and splashed over my forehead and into my hair. I pushed her off, letting her slump to the side, and looked at Joel to see if he was okay.

He kicked the biter in the face and trudged back from the shuffler. The shuffler came in fast. Joel slashed a Z across the face. Kicked back, making another Z drop. A rotter covered in rags reached for Joel.

Another loud shot, and one of the Zs that was after Joel went down in a heap.

A couple of shapes took form from the East. I looked, then did a double-take as they materialized, sun-high, blinding me. They strode like something out of a western.

Roz and Anna to the rescue.

Anna struggled to keep her arm crossed across her chest, but her good hand held a handgun. It boomed, and the shuffler that had been so persistent fell to the side like a wounded animal. It snarled, touched a wound on his leg, then skittered away on three limbs. Anna lifted the gun and aimed, but dropped the heavy barrel as the shuffler disappeared around the corner of a building.

I rolled over and found my feet. Then I found my wrench. Cleanup duty was almost fun.

13:50 hours approximate
Location: Vista

Turned out that the place had been surrounded by Zs. Anna and Roz decided to move a few blocks to the East, but Roz had been smart and left us a note: the flapping piece of paper I'd been trying to reach. When the shuffler had led his little army of dumbshits into our temporary Fortress, Roz had backed the camper up and moved down a few blocks.

Roz helped carry some of the supplies. I put the half-case of beef stew over my shoulder and ignored the rumbling in my gut.

We trudged back to the camper and found it under the overhang of a house that was long since ransacked, and partially burned-out. One of the walls had a hole big enough to drive a motorcycle through, and was surrounded by ash-covered belongings. Whoever had fled that place had come back to gather anything they could salvage, then left sans foreclosure sign.

We didn't have long before daylight was gone, and I planned for us to be on the road as soon as possible.

It was silent until we were close enough to see the drawn curtains covering the camper's small windows. Joel went first and inspected the site to make sure no one had taken an unwelcome interest while we were gone. He moved through the house, and then did a sweep of the camper.

When Christy and the dog appeared in the camper doorway, I finally breathed a sigh of relief.

#

13:50 hours approximate
Location: Vista

An hour later we'd pulled off a side road and parked under some trees. We warmed up a couple of cans of stew, and as much as I'd promised myself I'd eat slowly, I ended up wolfing down my portion. Some canned mixed vegetables got added to the mix. In a small pot, Roz had made a few cups of rice. It was the most filling meal I'd had in a week.

I wanted to take a nap, but we had business to take care of.

#

13:50 hours approximate
Location: Vista

Anna tossed back a pair of painkillers, looked at the pills in the bottom of the little brown bottle, and added two more. She downed a bottle of water and then looked at us expectantly.

"Wish this was vodka or something," she said. "What will they do to me besides numb the pain?"

"Oh you're gonna feel really good in about half an hour. Those are Percocets, you've heard of Oxy, right?"

"Yeah."

"Same thing. Get ready to feel a little better about the apocalypse in about twenty minutes,"

Roz said.

"It'll be over soon, baby." I tried to sound reassuring.

"Call me baby again and I'll jam a pain pill up your ass just before I kick you up and down the camper."

"Damn, I like it when you talk dirty."

Anna looked away, but a half-smile curled her lips. She lay on the bed with her arm exposed. The wound was an angry red. Hot, puckered infection would kill her if we didn't get it under control. Roz thought that the best way to take care of Anna was to get the bullet out.

I took a few steps away and motioned for Roz to join me. I leaned over to talk to her, and kept my voice low.

"You know how to do this, right?" I asked.

"In theory, sure. I'll dig around and pull out the bullet. It's gonna hurt like a motherfucker."

"You've done something like this before?" I asked.

"No, Creed, I have never dug a fucking bullet out of someone's arm. I've never taken a bullet out of anything. I saw a doctor take a lead pellet out of a dog's flank, but we had to put the little puppy out for the extraction. We can't do that with Anna--no drugs in our possession that can do that. Besides, there's no way to monitor her in case her blood pressure drops or she goes into shock."

"The Percocets should work, right?"

"It'll help put her in a haze. I don't know, it

might work. It also depends on how much pain she can tolerate. She's pretty tough, so it might be a walk in the park. I really wish we had some kind of a local."

"Local?"

"Shot. Some Lidocaine, assuming I could get a hypodermic needle and put it deep enough into the wound."

I glanced over my shoulder at Anna, who turned white, which was about what I wanted to do.

"Just fucking get it over with," Anna groaned. "You're about as quiet as a cat in heat. Seriously, Jackson, your whisper is the way normal people talk."

"Hey, I'm trying to be sensitive to your needs."

"Jesus fucking Christ," Anna sighed.

We pulled chairs around Anna and talked about little things while we waited for the pills to kick in. Anna didn't have to tell me. I saw the glazed look come over her eyes pretty quickly.

"Okay. I kinda get it now," she said.

"Get what?" I asked.

"Why people get addicted to this shit."

Roz and I had found enough half-ass tools to do the deed. I'd found a pair of tweezers with a spring between the tines and managed to flatten the pointed ends with a rock and some oil.

Then Roz made me boil the shit out them.

The RV had turned up a number of useful goodies, like a bottle of rubbing alcohol, some peroxide, and small sewing kit. We found a small first aid kit in the RV, too, but the innards had been replaced with dice.

"Are you going to sew up the wound after the bullet's out?" I asked Roz.

"No, because if there's an infection we'll end up containing it. Better to just put a bandage on so I can irrigate the wound. Wish I had saline solution, but that water you boiled will be the next best thing."

"You're going to pour water in the hole?" I asked.

"Yeah," Roz said.

I got my degree in medical knowledge from watching TV, so I didn't argue.

"Can't you use some of the alcohol?" I asked.

"Don't you even think about pouring alcohol into my arm," Anna said, and then stared at the ceiling.

"We won't, because it could damage the tissue. Better to clean it, cover it, and feed her antibiotics."

Roz poured alcohol on her hands and then let them air dry.

"Should I do that?" I asked, nodding at the booze.

"Keep your hands away from her wound. No telling where they've been," Roz said.

"Yeah, Creed, you dirty bastard," Anna laughed. "No telling where they've been."

"Can you sit up, Anna? I need to be able to drain the area."

"Sure. Drain away," Anna said.

Roz used a small soda bottle with a hole punched in the cap to squeeze water into the hole. Yellowish fluid came out.

"Okay. I'm going to feel around the wound and try to locate the bullet, as well as any fragments. This will probably hurt."

"I don't really care right now. I'm high as a kite," she grinned.

Roz looked at me. "Hold her."

I leaned over and put a hand on her shoulder and then my arm across her chest. Roz moved beside me and pulled the bandage off of Anna's wound.

"I told you that I'm not into that stuff, Creed," Anna said, and then giggled. I didn't envy her when the high wore off. She was going to sleep and wake up hurting, but we didn't have painkillers to spare.

"Yeah, I'll keep that in mind," I said.

Roz started by probing the wound with her fingers. She didn't press hard but as she explored, Anna's body language changed.

"I can feel that but it's not too bad," Anna said and took a deep breath.

"It's going to get worse. Sorry," Roz said.

I had to look away when she stuck the tweezers in the wound.

"Motherfuck!" Anna said and nearly bolted up off the bed.

I held her down, but I didn't like it. Anna was

slight but she was powerfully built, so I had to hold her none too gently.

"I'm sorry. I almost had it, try not to move."

I glanced over and then regretted it. Blood oozed out of the wound and ran down the back of Anna's arm. The hole was small, but it looked red and infected. I'd seen a lot of nasty stuff out in the z-poc world, but it was different when the damage was on someone I cared for.

"That can't get, like, *infected*, right?" I said to Roz and lifted my eyebrows for emphasis.

"Of course it can, Creed. It may be infected now."

"That's not what I…"

"He means can the zombie stuff get into my wound," Anna said between clenched teeth.

"I fucking hope not," Roz said.

Roz dug in the wound and then pulled the tweezers up. Anna bucked under me.

"Shit, I almost had it."

"Let me go, Creed," Anna said. "I'll do this myself."

I looked for confirmation from Roz.

"*Now*, goddamn it!" Anna swore.

Roz nodded.

I lifted the pressure off her body and stood up.

Anna reached across her body and grasped her upper arm.

The door rocked open and in stepped Joel Kelly. He took one look at the blood and his face dropped.

Anna grunted. She squeezed the skin around the wound, teeth clenched, lips in a snarl. She let out something like a growl and then pressed upward.

The bullet popped out of the wound and fell on the towels.

My mouth dropped open.

Roz grinned.

"Positively badass, Sails. Positively badass," Joel said.

I felt like passing out.

#

All Hands on Deck

07:30 hours approximate
Location: Just outside of Oceanside

Another day, another headache.

That's not a metaphor. For the last few days I'd woken up with a headache that started at the base of my skull, spread up my head, and then ended with a pounding sensation behind my eyes. I tried and tried to ignore the pain.

Today the thumping was bad enough to remind me of my epic drinking days: fun times that had ended just a couple of months ago, thanks to the zombie fucking apocalypse. It wasn't that there was a lack of booze--there was plenty, if you looked in enough houses. It was Joel Kelly, who ended up being my personal AA and sponsor all wrapped up into one.

"Get drunk, get dead," Kelly had said after I spun the top off a bottle of cheap whiskey.

I'd procured the drink from a rambler a few days before, and had been saving it.

"Not if I get whiskey dick."

"Gonna get dead is what you're gonna get. Can't stay frosty if you're drunk off your ass."

"A little sip or two isn't the end of the world," I'd argued.

"This *is* the end of the world, and there ain't no coming back. No waking up in the brig cause you assaulted an officer. No waking up in your rack reaching for a half dozen aspirin. It's lights out like a mo' fucka."

I hated to admit it, but Joel had made a lot of sense. With very few exceptions I'd been clean and sober since then. Maybe not so much on the clean part. The last shower I'd had was one very cold one with Anna Sails the night we'd added Frosty to our crew. Since then it's been baby-wipe baths and splashing water under the pits from time to time.

But this headache. Damn. It was like someone was pounding nails into the back of my neck and skull.

It was time to be a baby.

07:45 hours approximate Location: Just outside of Oceanside

"Roz. My head is killing me again," I said.

"Your face is killing me," Joel quipped.

"Man. If I wasn't in so much pain I'd have a comeback that would put you down for the count." I put my hands to the sides of my head, hoping to keep my head from bursting open.

"How much water have you been drinking?" Roz asked.

"I don't know. Enough, I guess," I said.

"Drink more," Roz said.

"Yeah. You can't get dehydrated," Christy said.

Christy had been walking Frosty and had just returned to the camper. She was dressed in jeans and a beat-up sweater. If I wasn't mistaken, the oversized and over-color-saturated top had been retrieved from the hotel we'd taken over with the mercenaries a few weeks ago.

"I'm not that thirsty."

"You need water. It's probably a headache from being dehydrated. You have to be careful, Creed," Christy cautioned.

Maybe she was right. While I ho-hummed, she unscrewed the lid on our water supply: a large, clear plastic container, and poured some into a sports bottle with a screw top. We had a bunch of those from raiding a store a few days ago. Most were pink, and that was the color she tossed me.

I sipped the tepid water and found it to be refreshing, even if it had a weird flavor--like silt and dirt--but it also tasted old, and had a plastic undercurrent. Not that I was a water connoisseur, but I wouldn't drink this stuff with my pinky up.

Thing is, you get used to hunting for something to drink, and when you find it you suck it down like there's no tomorrow. I hadn't been doing enough of that.

We'd need to filter more pretty soon, since we were down to a few gallons. That was tedious, but I'd taught Christy how to make a water filter out of a soda bottle, sand, and rocks. She'd made half a dozen of the devices, and used them on a daily basis.

"Drink," Christy commanded.

Roz and Joel had been conferring. As morning came on, they'd decided to move out. We were about ten miles from Pendleton, but those miles might as well have been walking distance for as slow as we were moving.

The confines of our portable house had become a breeding ground for arguments. Stick four and a half people together in a little space and they were bound to get grumpy with each other. I was ready for a place to stretch out.

We'd come to the agreement that we needed to rest up another day, because Anna, for all of her badassery, was still in pain. She was taking her antibiotics and painkillers, but she had also developed a low-grade fever.

"We're moving out," Joel said.

He moved to the door and pushed aside the shitty little rag of a curtain. Joel peered outside for a few seconds, then readied his gun. He cracked the door, and slid out like death with an assault rifle. He moved around the sides of the vehicle and then gestured. Roz slipped out, gun at the ready.

"Those two," I said fondly.

"What about them?" Christy asked.

"I don't know. I can't read them most of the time, but they have a thing and it's cool."

"Of course they have a thing. Everyone has a thing except me," Christy said.

"You don't want a boyfriend during this mess. Wait until we're settled in somewhere. You'll meet a nice boy who's good at head shots."

"I'm good at heads shots, dude," she smirked. "I don't need a boy to save me."

"You're right," I smiled. "You're a crack shot now. You'd probably scare the boys off."

Christy nodded and then went back to nursing the filters as they dripped water into cans.

The camper lurched forward and I was nearly thrown off my feet. Who the hell was driving up there?

I took a seat next to Anna and pressed a wet cloth to her head.

"You know that is really irritating, right?" she said.

"This is what they do in the movies when someone has a fever."

"Creed. The last thing I want is warm water dripping onto my pillow."

I lifted the wash cloth and wiped water off her forehead. I leaned over and kissed her in the same spot. Her features softened for a second, but then her mask returned.

"Sorry. I was just trying to be helpful."

"Help Christy with the water. There's a lot to

filter, and you getting dehydrated is going to put a dent in what we have," she said, and closed her eyes.

"That's still up for debate. I'm calling this a normal headache, like your everyday variety, 'my head fucking hurts', headache. I'm drinking water. Jesus."

Anna opened her eyes. "What color was your pee this morning?"

"What?"

"Don't act like a twelve-year-old. We've seen each other. So what was your pee color: was it light or dark?"

"It was dark, why?"

"Because you're fucking dehydrated. Now go make some clean water and drink it while I lay here and try not to throw up. My skin itches, Creed. It's the painkillers. I hate this feeling."

"I'm sorry, baby," I said, unsure if I should touch her again.

"It's fine. I just need to be better. I need to stop the Percocets. But Roz is going to irrigate my wound later, and it's gonna hurt like a mother."

I nodded, touched the blanket that bunched up on her knee, and patted it gently.

"And stop calling me baby."

I rose with a sigh.

08:15 hours approximate
Location: Just outside of Oceanside

Christy had been busy gathering water from a nearby house. A week ago Joel and I had figured out that we could drain water from hot water tanks after the place we were raiding had already been picked clean. The water had been brackish and smelled none too clean, but our homemade filters made that shit taste like almost as good as low-rent Cristal.

We carefully poured the water into filters and waited while it seeped through the sand, charcoal, and fabric. They hung under the kitchen sink, and had tubes trailing into a large plastic container.

I poured out about sixteen ounces and drained it in a few long gulps--and then felt guilty for being such a hog.

Christy smiled at me and handed over another bottle. I sipped this one like a reasonably thirsty dude.

"Doing okay?" I asked her.

"Yeah. Just bored."

"We found some magazines in the last house. I put a stack near the door."

"I know, but it's all old news. Who cares which celebrity is getting married or which one has a baby bump? They're all gone now anyway."

"Maybe we should write a story together."

"I'm not that creative, Creed. You're the writer."

"Not much of one. I just write down our daily adventures, and I'm not very good at it," I said.

"You're really good. I read the first log book and thought it was great. Lots of misspellings, but it didn't bother me."

"I'll hire an editor when the world is restored," I chuckled. "You should ask before reading them."

"You and Kelly were gone for a while, so Anna and I looked at them. Anna said you exaggerated a lot."

I coughed.

"But she said you were kind of a badass." Christy leaned close. "She told me not to tell you that."

I looked over my shoulder and found Anna's eyes on mine. I winked, but her face was stone. Then she closed her eyes and rolled onto her side.

"I guess it doesn't matter. You can read them. I'll put this conversation in the new log book."

"Oh jeez."

The camper took a hard turn, then slowed.

Last night we'd been laying up in an open parking lot that was filled with ransacked cars. Our vehicle was as far away from the Walmart as possible while still leaving at least two exits. We didn't bother with the store, because the doors were shattered and carts and debris littered the entryway.

Someone had spray-painted obscenities over the front of the building. Others had even seen fit to crawl up on the roof and hack at the bright blue signs, leaving just a few letters intact so that it spelled out ALMA.

I was pretty sure people were camped on top of the building, but we didn't bother to investigate. If they stayed out of our shit, we'd stay out of theirs. Joel and I walked the perimeter of the camper, then ranged out to check for anything of interest, but as suspected, the few abandoned cars had long since been stripped of anything useful.

"That's a good idea: build a fort on top of a big-ass Walmart. It's easily defensible and you could hide out from Zs pretty easy," I said.

"Yeah, until the place is surrounded by five thousand fools looking for flesh. Remember when we fled our first Fortress?" Joel said, making sense as usual.

"They must know the trick, then, because whoever is up there isn't surrounded."

"One mistake, and it's undeadville, as you like to say. Like kicking over a soup can with those big feet of yours."

"Gimme a break, man," I said.

"Let's head out," Joel answered.

The truck rumbled to life and then lurched forward. I got a hand out to steady myself, and then stood with popping knee joints.

Christy grabbed a couple of old magazines and put them on the table, then hopped up to page through them. I grabbed one and joined her, but within a few minutes I was also bored, because Christy was right: these things didn't matter anymore.

Next chance we got, I was going to bring back a

stack of paperbacks to help pass the time.

I laid out our weapons and inspected each and every one. If Joel had taught me one thing, it was that we needed to keep our guns ready for action. Christy was a quick study, and pitched in to help. Together we stripped guns, ran rags over the moving parts, and lubricated them from a can of motor oil.

Christy smiled more than once as we sat in companionable silence, so I smiled back. When we were done, I slipped the Springfield XDM 9mm into its holster.

The next few hours weren't so bad after all.

###

16:15 hours approximate
Location: Just outside of Oceanside

After bumping along back roads at a crawl for several hours, Joel brought the truck to a halt.

I'd been eyeing the world from inside the camper while we bounced along. It wasn't just the main roads; even the back alleys and paths had been littered with debris and abandoned cars. Bodies--always bodies, most unmoving--blocked us at points. I'd gotten used to jumping out of our vehicle and helping Joel move the dead out of the way, or bashing in the heads of rotters before dragging them off to the side.

Now that we'd stopped, I looked outside and found that we were near a housing development that was somewhat secluded, thanks to a tall line of cypress trees. The place looked like a country club in the making. Half-finished homes lay next to completed two-story stucco- and particle-board-sided buildings.

I stepped out of the camper and joined Joel and Roz.

"Nice place you found," I said.

"I think Oceanside is just a few miles west of our location. Tomorrow we should see Pendleton," Joel said.

"You think we're going to find the base operational?" I had to ask. We'd had this goal for weeks, and now that it was within reach, I wondered if we would find what we were even looking for. The camp could be a graveyard for all we knew.

"That's the hope, brother. That's the hope," Joel said.

"What now?"

"We need a place to sleep. Gonna take a look around. You two scout around but stay close. I'll get on top of the camper and cover you, but if you see Zs, you come back and we'll leave," Joel said.

"Aye aye, captain," I said with a smirk.

He clambered up the side of the camper to the roof. Joel stood up and scanned the area, hand shading his eyes as he took up lookout duty.

Roz and I explored but didn't find anything except homes with kicked in doors--assuming they had even been completed. I thought I saw a pair of eyes peeking out from one house, but decided not to investigate any further.

The largest problem was a pile of people who'd been dragged into the street and shot in their heads. From the state of decay--that was, rot and shredded clothing that might have been gnawed at by feral dogs--it was hard to tell if they'd been alive when they were killed or had already been Zs.

We found a heap of bodies with a row of decapitated heads next to it. They were stacked up in an obscene pyramid. Darkened and in some cases blood-filled eye sockets, from which dried-out and damned eyes stared back.

We dragged bodies off to the side, Joel with a stubborn look on his face, me with a red bandana wrapped around mine. It didn't really help to alleviate the smell, but it made me feel like I was making the effort.

A mini-horde of moaners found us just as we cleared the road, so we got back in the truck and drove on. No reason to stick around and try to slaughter them when they weren't a threat.

After we finished our sweep, Joel located a house with a carport and backed in, because with night falling, the development seemed the best place to call home for the night.

"Looks like Joel found us a pretty swanky place," I said to Anna.

I inspected her wound. It looked good, as far as my untrained eye could tell. It was hot around the entry point, but I suspected that was okay. I'd ask Roz later.

"We need another location to sleep that isn't this cramped camper, especially since Joel snores," I said.

"So do you, Creed. You snore like a goddamn train. Get me some fucking earplugs the next time you make a supply run."

"Earplugs? You wouldn't hear the Zs coming," I said, and made claws out of my hands, lifting them in my best approximation of a zombie.

"You're scarier when you snore," she said.

I rolled my eyes and lurched forward as the truck came to a stop. Joel cranked it to the right and then backed up again. Christy rose and looked out the window. She carried her snub-nosed revolver in one hand. I had to admire the kid. She'd gone from a sad and awkward teen to a tougher and still-awkward teen ready to pop a Z in the head if they got too close.

Anna pushed the sheet aside. She wasn't wearing much, and my eyes traveled up and down her legs. It'd been a week since we'd been intimate, and I missed looking at her.

Anna followed my eyes and blew out a breath. "Perv."

"I've been staring at walls for days. You're a sight, baby," I said.

Anna tugged her pants on and got to her feet. She leaned over and put her hand on my shoulder. I reached for her, but she shook her head.

"Sorry. Just a little dizzy. I'm okay now."

Joel opened the door. "We're here, kids. I hope you ain't been fighting back here."

Christy giggled and slipped past him. Anna wrapped her belt around her waist and slid the Smith & Wesson M&P R8 into the holster. She moved to the door, and Joel helped her down.

I grabbed my wrench and joined them.

16:30 hours approximate
Location: Just outside of Oceanside

The house had two entry points, not including the windows. It was two stories, and the paint hadn't been applied on the inside or out. There was a For Sale sign driven into the ground outside. The lawn was dirt where grass would have been layered in long strips. A few shrubs had been planted, but most of them were now wilted.

Place like this was probably kept up until a potential buyer happened along. With the current drought conditions in California it wasn't a surprise. Should say *former* drought conditions. Without thirty-eight million people constantly showering, watering lawns, and filling pools, it stood to reason that there was now enough water to go around. All we had to do was find a mountain, and we'd have an unlimited supply.

"Pools," I said.

"Bars," Joel said.

"What?"

"Thought we were just saying random fucking words, Creed."

"I was just thinking--California is filled with pools. We should find one that isn't too stagnant and stick a hose in. Siphon up a bunch of water and filter or boil it."

"Damn, Skippy, you're pretty smart for a squid," Joel said.

I shot him the finger.

"That's a good idea. Maybe tomorrow we can scout some of the houses and look for water. It's been relatively cool. The problem is all the chlorine. I don't know if we can filter it out. Plus the pools have been sitting unattended for close to two months. I'm not even sure if we should risk it," Roz said.

Joel nodded. He slung his AR-15 around his neck on his two-point sling and double-checked his sidearm.

Joel and Roz walked the perimeter while Anna, Christy and I kept an eye out for Zs and moved our supplies near the back door. I tapped a few windows and then moved away. No faces--living or dead--appeared.

The backyard butted up to a small wooded area that made me think twice about this location.

"You sure that's safe?" I said and pointed at the trees.

"I figure it will be a last resort. We can move faster than Zs if we have to run. The trees'll slow

113

them down. There's another house that's done and has a better view all around, but I saw something moving inside."

"I don't feel like a Z hunt tonight," I said.

About the worst thing in the world was going through a house, clearing it, and hoping we weren't surprised by some crafty rotter who'd shamble out of a closet while we had our backs turned.

When we reached the rear of the house I tried the door, but it was double-locked. I pushed, but Joel motioned for me to join him.

"See that window?" He pointed.

"Yeah, but how am I going to get up there? I don't see a ladder."

"I'm going, you weigh more than me."

"What's that got to do with anything?" I said.

"'Cause you're gonna give me a boost."

Joel put his assault rifle on the ground and motioned for me to cup my hands.

"You kidding? I'm not sure I can lift you with all that damn gear."

"One way to find out, sailor. I could climb up on your shoulders if that makes you feel better. Just stand there like a big-ass tree."

"Oh for Christ's sake," I said and cupped my hands.

Joel put his boot in my improvised sling and his hands on my shoulders.

"On three," he said.

We counted and he jumped. I felt like I was

flinging him into the air, but he caught the edge of the roof. He nearly ripped the gutter off, but managed to pull himself up until his legs were dangling. He dragged himself over, then flipped around and motioned toward me. I handed Joel his assault rifle and backed away to watch.

Joel moved to the window and stared inside for a few seconds. He pressed the jamb and lifted. The portal opened without a sound.

Joel slipped inside and then was gone from sight.

###

16:45 hours approximate
Location: Just outside of Oceanside

I slid out the Springfield XDM and waited. The gun felt good in my hand, but it wasn't my only weapon. I didn't go anywhere without my trusty eight-pound wrench, so it was hanging uncomfortably under my arm.

I half expected Joel's rifle to start barking out 5.56 rounds, but he reached the back door, unbolted it, and swung it open.

"Let's do a full sweep. I checked the bedroom I entered but the rest are waiting. The stairs and the entry to the kitchen are clear. I didn't go through all the closets yet. Stay frosty," he said.

Frosty lifted her head at the sound of her name.

"Get 'em, girl," I said and let her go.

Frosty dashed into the house and ran toward a

back room.

I trailed behind Joel and followed his lead. One of the worst things about entering a new house is looking in all the rooms and doorways. We'd learned early on that folks couldn't kill a loved one. They preferred to lock them in a little space, presumably to wait for a cure or just so they didn't have to put up with the moans and biting.

Joel moved through the house, checking and clearing each area. When we entered rooms I kept my eyes on the corners and his back. The thing about the dead is: they might be hanging around, staring at a wall, and you wouldn't even know it until they were on you.

The floors weren't finished, but the concrete had a layer of padding. Carpet lay in huge rolls in the dining room and wood strips were stacked up in another corner. Fading sunlight lit the room from an abundance of windows, creating a space that was easy to inspect.

We hit every closet and room, looked in half-finished bathrooms and in cabinets and pantries. I expected the upstairs to have a few Zs, but the rooms were also clear and as bare as the downstairs.

We found some supplies and a surprise in a closet: paint, paint thinner, masking tape, a couple of rulers, some power tools, and other small contractor items. A toolbox revealed hand tools and a few boxes of screws, bolts, and nuts.

One of the tools--a cordless drill--was stuck in a

man's head. His body was decayed and partially mummified. It was hard to tell if someone had killed him or if he'd done it himself. I considered what I'd do if I was bitten and all I had was a fucking power drill. Would I have the nerve to drive it into my own head?

Frosty growled at the body. I rubbed her head and got a lick for my efforts.

"Damn, that dude reeks," Joel said.

"Let's get the stuff we can use, and then leave him to his tomb. He's not going to bother us," I said.

"We're at that point, huh? Fucking corpse in the house and we're just gonna leave it?" Joel said.

"What else should we do, drag him outside and do a burial? Nah, man, I've seen enough corpses and body parts to last me three lifetimes."

"Let's not tell the ladies, eh?" Joel said.

"Sexist asshole," I laughed. "None of them is squeamish."

"I was thinking of Christy. Girl's seen enough bodies, rot, and Zs to last three lifetimes. No sense her worrying about a body in the house."

"Yeah, man. I get it. Well, looks like we got a home for a night," I said. "What do you think a place like this costs?"

"Before the Zs? Probably more money than you and I make in a few years. After the apocalypse? Shit's free."

We took out anything that might be useful and moved it into the kitchen.

One thing was for damn sure: I was looking forward to stretching out.

#

17:30 hours approximate
Location: Just outside of Oceanside

I brought Frosty along when I moved the truck behind the house. She investigated the unfinished yard for a few minutes before finding the perfect place to take a dump. Christy stayed close to the dog, and praised her when she didn't run off. Frosty was loyal to us first, and teasing/chasing Zs second. Still, she paused a few times to sniff the air, and looked in the direction of the woods once or twice.

Joel and Roz moved food, the burner, and other gear inside the house. Anna picked up her bag and a couple of cans of food. I joined her and offered my arm, but she shook me off. She looked a bit dazed, but I suspected it was the drugs. Her short hair was frazzled and she looked like she needed a week off in a tropical vacation getaway. Her body language was tense--that was the best word for it. She ran her hands over the stock of the handgun at her side more than once.

"She spooked?" Anna nodded toward Frosty.

"Not sure. Maybe there's a maimed Z back in the woods somewhere."

Anna walked to the corner of the yard. She petted Frosty and waited, head moving back and forth as she scanned the copses.

The dog must have gotten bored, because she sat down and scratched her neck for a few seconds, and then galloped back to me. I rubbed her head and assured her she was a dyed in the wool killer.

We moved gear into the house, just enough for the night, and set up camp in the middle of the kitchen. The entryway was open, but there was only one window. Joel and I cut off a big chunk of carpet and wedged it over the portal. No sense in advertising that we had taken up occupancy.

I checked the faucet over the sink, but no water came out. I found the valves and twisted the cold lever all the way to the right. To my surprise, water gurgled up the tubes. It came out in a trickle, but Christy was quick and got a bucket under the stream until it ran out. We got about two gallons. I tasted it and found it stale, but grabbed a mug from our belongings and gulped it down.

"Don't want to clean it first?" Roz asked.

"It just tastes like pipes. Water's been sitting there but it's clean," I said.

Christy didn't look convinced, and told us she'd take it out to the camper and run it through our filtering system.

"Take Frosty," I said. She nodded and ducked out of the house.

"It's good to stretch out," Joel said.

"Yeah. Good to get some life back in our legs," Roz nodded.

Joel caught her looking at him and gave a small nod. He rose and together they went to "investigate" the house.

Anna pulled a sleeping bag out of her pack and rolled it out flat. She crawled inside and zipped it up.

"Room for me in there?" I winked.

"Sorry. I'm running a fever and everything makes my skin crawl right now. Nothing personal, Creed," she said.

I nodded and took out the burner and a couple of cans of stew. Might as well eat our precious supplies while we had the opportunity. Tomorrow we'd arrive at the Marine base, if we weren't ambushed by shufflers, devoured by fucking zombies, or killed by marauders--or if we didn't succumb to some stupid disease that was out to do us in. That's what our lives had come to: running from all of the things that wanted to do us harm.

"I'm going to see if there's enough water for a good flush in the bathroom," I said.

"Great, Creed. If not, nail the door shut when you're done," Anna said.

20:40 hours approximate
Location: Just outside of Oceanside

We gathered in the tiny room and made a decent dinner: stew, canned beans, a can of creamed corn, and a few crackers. Anna said she was feeling better, so I sat next to her and tried to cheer her up with dumb stories of being young and overseas. I got the occasional half-smile out of her, but she wasn't really paying attention to me.

Roz and Joel rolled out sleeping mats and piled on a few blankets. Christy wrote in a journal-- something she'd seen me do every day, and something I'd encouraged.

Frosty rolled on her back and growled. Her tail swished back and forth while her tongue lolled out. She wanted to play, and nipped at my hand a few times while I rubbed her chest.

"Anyone want to play spades?" I asked.

Christy shook her head and went back to writing. Joel and Roz looked at each other, then shook their heads as well.

"Can't play with just two people," I said to myself.

"Play with yourself," Anna suggested.

I cracked a smile.

Christy and I played a few hands of high stakes five-card poker and I ended up owing her six million dollars. Just my luck. Last week she'd owed me fifteen million, give or take.

I know a lot of people probably love the quiet. I don't. I was used to the noise of the engine room, the hum of the pipes, steam, and the exhaust fans that blew air around the ship. I slept like a goddamn baby when I was out at sea. When I stayed in town I needed a fan cranked up to high just to doze off.

Out in Z land, I was lucky if I got more than four consecutive hours' worth of sleep. I was always on guard, and the quiet didn't help. Every time someone moved or sniffed or snored or burped or farted, it was like a bell rung next to my head. Exhaustion usually knocked me out, but today I was still on edge.

I tried relaxing and thinking of better times: times that involved beer and hookers in some overseas port. I thought of the night Anna and I had spent a few weeks ago. We'd taken an ice-cold shower together, and I for one had felt clean for the first time in ages.

Although she didn't want to share our sleeping bags, I'd laid mine out next to her.

I rolled over and looked at her. She looked peaceful for a change.

"What?" she whispered, opening one eye.

"Nothing. Just looking at you," I whispered back.

"Go to sleep, Creed. I'm beat," she said, and rolled over.

"Are you mad at me for something?"

"No, Jackson, I'm not mad at you. I just don't need a boyfriend right now and that's all there is to it. Now get some sleep."

I blew out a breath and rolled onto my back. The view of the ceiling didn't help. It was white, unfinished, and boring.

An hour later I still tossed and turned. Joel snored, and Roz snored quietly next to him. The pair had curled into each other and looked rather goddamn cozy.

Christy had dragged her sleeping pad across the floor and was facing the door. Earlier we'd drawn cards to see who would take first watch. Even though we tried to coddle Christy when we could, she insisted on being treated like an adult. She wanted to take watch every night, and she was good. Christy never dozed off and she rarely ever bugged us, unless she sensed a genuine threat.

I'd had increasingly bad insomnia as the weeks fled past, and tonight looked like it would be no different. I rose as silently as I could and lifted my backpack. I moved across the room and leaned over to whisper to Christy.

"Get some rest. I can't sleep, so I'll keep watch for the next few hours and then I'll wake Roz."

Christy nodded and wiped at her eyes. I suspected she'd been crying, but she hit me with a hard look that would have made Anna proud.

"Okay. Thanks," she said and rolled over.

I took my pack into the living room and sat with my back to a wall. Then I took out my journal and wrote for an hour.

#

12:30 hours approximate
Location: Just outside of Oceanside

My eyes were heavy and the thought of sleep was getting more and more attractive. I'd spent the last few hours alternating between writing and staring outside.

A couple of creepers had wandered past the house and then into the woods. I let them be. The pair found something on the ground--the carcass of a small animal--and they fought over it. Not much of a battle, because one of the Zs was missing most of an arm.

I wondered, not for the first time, what their story had been. Had they been married, had kids, were they working-class, were they nice to their families? So many people gone now, and what was the world going to be like in a year? Would we all be mindless, wandering ghouls?

I closed my eyes a couple of times to let them rest, because they burned. I yawned and decided I could probably sleep.

Roz rose grumpy and took her place on watch. I curled up next to Anna as close as I could get without touching her sleeping bag, and closed my eyes. Within moments I drifted off.

###

In the Crosshairs

08:35 hours Approximate
Location: Just outside of Oceanside

I woke to the sound of laughter.

Christy was playing in the living room with Frosty. I rubbed grit out of my eyes and rolled over to stare at the ceiling. I was the only one in the kitchen. The amount of sun streaming in through the window told me I'd done something I hadn't done in a long time: I'd slept in.

I peeked around the space that divided the two rooms and saw the source of Christy's laughter. She had the dog lying on the floor and was trying to teach her how to roll over. Frosty didn't seem to think too much of the game. She lay with her legs splayed in the air, her tail wagging across the floor while her tongue lolled out the side of her mouth.

The room had unfinished walls and a lack of carpeting. The floor was concrete, but Christy had broken into some of the padding and rolled it out for Frosty to sleep on.

I jumped when someone tapped at the front

door, in a pattern consisting of three quick knocks and then two knocks spaced farther apart. Christy hopped up. Frosty scrambled to her side and got to her feet, her demeanor changed instantly from playful pup to "I'm going to rip someone a new one".

Christy peeked out the bay windows, then smiled and nodded. The door opened, and in strolled Joel Kelly and Roz. They carried a number of tools, some lumber, and a bag of screws or nails.

"Morning, sunshine," Roz said.

I nodded. Christy turned and shot me a smile, so I smiled back. Not hard to do when faced with her sunny disposition. We were safe for a while, and it had rubbed off on her.

Joel and Roz quietly placed their newly-acquired items around the living room. Roz removed a piece of paper from her pocket, and she and Joel studied the sheet.

"What's going on?" I asked.

"We're going to fortify this place and try to rest up for a few days. Tired of being on the run, bro," Joel said.

"What about Pendleton?"

"It'll still be there. Or maybe it's already gone. Rushing down there now while we're exhausted, Anna's hurt, and you're needing ten hours of sleep means that we are not an effective fighting unit," Joel said.

"So what, we're going to board up the windows and call this Fortress Mark III?"

"Something like that. This subdivision is half-finished, so a lot of families hadn't moved in yet. North of here a few homes that look occupied. We didn't bother investigating."

"So we're not getting a welcome to the neighborhood basket?" I deadpanned.

Roz chuckled.

"I'd love some cupcakes," Joel sighed.

"Don't talk about cupcakes. I haven't had fresh-baked *anything* in months, so you're making me drool," Christy said.

"Something bothers me about this place," I said.

"What, no store set up for bartering yet?" Joel said.

"It's the lack of people. This place isn't finished yet, sure, not a lot of families would be moved in, but why didn't other survivors take over and fortify? The place backs up to a small hill, the houses are close together, it seems like the perfect opportunity to build a community and keep it guarded."

"Thinking like a warrior, huh? I'll be honest, I had the same thought. What's missing is any kind of lawns. The backyards are barely in and who knows if anything can grow in that soil. If we stayed we'd need a garden at the very least. Grow potatoes and carrots. But California's been in a hell of a drought, so getting water in would be a bitch." Joel removed his ball cap and scratched his head.

"Maybe it's just been overlooked. Think about

how many people the virus has taken. Think about how many are dead or roaming the streets. If only a percentage of the population is still alive, they have a lot of places to hide," Anna chimed in.

"Personally, if I wanted to become a warlord and rule a little kingdom I'd take over a fucking Costco. Big-ass brick building, lots of food, just need a few guys to keep it safe and sound," Joel said.

"And a bunch of scantily-clad women to call your harem?" Roz asked.

"If I'm a warlord of Costco, you bet your ass," Joel said.

Roz, characteristically, smacked his arm. "You keep thinking like that and I'll punch you into tomorrow, Joel Kelly."

I stifled a laugh.

"What, you asked," Joel said. "Peace, baby. I'm just playing."

Roz crossed her arms over her chest.

"Damn, Joel. That's like some stupid shit *I'd* say," I chuckled.

"Joel, Warlord of Costco. Has a certain ring," he said.

Frosty wandered to the back of the house and scratched at the door.

"Gotta take a dump?" I asked her.

Christy rolled her eyes and took Frosty into the backyard.

"Keep her quiet," I said.

"I don't think there are any zombies back

there," Christy said as she stood in the doorway.

"How do you know?"

"Because they would have come if they heard your snoring," Christy said, and then closed the door as she stepped onto the back porch.

Anna strolled down the stairs. She wore camouflage pants and a t-shirt she'd picked out of one of our various bags. The shirt bore a grinning cat on a cartoon background.

She had a smile on her face.

"I don't even know what to say right now," I said to Anna.

Christy chased Frosty into the yard.

"Don't say a word," Anna said.

"But that shirt and that smile. Are you happy to see me?"

Anna sat next to me. She inspected a couple of scratches on my face and arms while I admired her sunny disposition. She'd either cleaned up in our small supply of water or she'd found some baby wipes along the way. She held her wounded arm next to her body, and when I reached out to inspect the injury she pulled away with an "I'm fine, Creed."

"So what's the plan for fortifying this place? Board up the doors?" I asked.

"If we board up everything, then someone may wonder what we're hoarding in here. We'll reinforce the door, but we need to keep the lights to a minimum. Avoid the windows if you can help it."

"What if no one bothers us?" I asked.

"What if monkeys fly out of my butt?" Roz said.

Joel snorted.

"The likelihood that we're going to be safe here for a few days is decent. The fact that Zs will find us is undeniable. Don't get too comfortable, folks," Joel said, looking between the members of our group.

"Is the truck prepped in case we need to make a quick getaway?"

"Yeah. Roz and I found a tarp to cover the truck, but if anyone gets too damn curious, they'll find the vehicle," Joel said.

"Good enough for Government work, I guess," I said.

Roz and Joel left on another scouting run. Anna stayed by my side but didn't say anything, so I leaned against the wall and enjoyed the companionable silence.

"I can't stay with you guys," she said, breaking the silence a few minutes later.

"What do you mean?"

"As soon as we find Bright Star I'm going to have to leave. I have responsibilities."

"To what? The world's gone now. Nothing but the dead and a few survivors scrounging for food. When it's all gone what are people going to do? Bright Star and the notion of any kind of functioning Government went out the window weeks ago."

"That's where you're wrong, Creed. There were contingency plans, and I believe we have a functioning Government, but they have been reduced. It's a matter of reestablishing bases and carving out our place in this new world. That's why they need me."

"Is this a paying job, this whole rebuilding-the-world thing?" I asked.

"I guess we're all owed some back pay. What are you going to do with a few months' worth of salary?" she asked.

"You're changing the subject."

"I'm turning it to something fun. You're so goddamn morose sometimes, Creed. You have this way of being a smartass and making everyone laugh, but half the time you're so depressed I wonder if you're going to slit your wrists," Anna said.

"Name one thing that doesn't suck now," I challenged her.

"Friends."

That got a half-smirk.

"The fact that you owe me seventeen million dollars from our last round of poker," she said.

"Any chance I can work that off another way?"

"We'll talk later tonight, Creed. I may have something you can do for me," she said, and hit me with a smile.

My day was starting to look better.

###

After Anna and I had our talk, I rose and grumped around for a half an hour, wishing more than anything that I had an energy drink or a gallon of coffee. A couple of weeks ago we'd found some packs of instant Starbucks coffee, but I'd kept them tucked deep inside my backpack and managed to make them last for a few days.

Even mixed with cold water, tasting grainy and undissolved, I'd treated them like fucking gold. I'd even thought about snorting the damn stuff for a rush. Probably end up with a headache and brown-colored snot.

Christy had filtered about a liter of water so I drank down a cup, then greedily drank another. I'd make it up to her by helping her filter more water later in the day.

I moved to the rear door and watched Christy and Frosty play. They'd found a stick, and the dog was running around, alternating between playing fetch and playing 'try to catch me'. She had a devious look in her eye every couple of times she brought the twig to Christy. Christy would reach for the stick, and Frosty would dance back and shake her head while her tail flopped from side to side.

I opened the door and stepped onto the partially-finished porch.

I sat down and Frosty, seeing me, dropped the stick and dashed up the stairs. She puppy-attacked me for a few minutes of mock play that involved trying to grab my sleeve and pull me into the yard. I rubbed the dog's head, and when she tired of that she dropped to her side and rolled on her back.

Christy took a seat next to Frosty and rubbed her belly while I did the same.

"Are we going to stay here for a while?" Christy asked.

"I don't think so. It's not safe to hang out in one location for more than a day or two. When Joel and I first got to San Diego we managed to hold out for almost a week. The Zs were still fairly new, and we didn't have a lot of crazies out trying to steal our stuff."

"Do you think someone will bother us here?"

"Hard to say. It's not like we know the neighborhood. Joel's got a plan to reinforce the place. If we have to, we'll just bug out. The camper's ready and we have a quarter tank of gas."

"How far will that get us?"

"Not very far, but far enough for now," I said. "If we run out there's a lot of cars we can siphon from. Problem is, gas gets old when it sits around, and might not be useable in a few months."

"What else won't be useable? I'm worried about stuff like supplies. They won't last forever, and we can only break into so many houses before there are no more canned goods sitting around."

"I guess we learn how to garden, and hunt

deer," I said.

"Is there a plan B?"

"Smartass."

Frosty stopped wagging her tail and shot to her feet. She stared into the woods that surrounded the backyard. She growled low in her throat, but then settled back down.

"Something back there?" Christy asked.

She stood and walked into the yard.

"Could be a Z that's stuck. We'll keep an eye out. If Frosty is on guard, I think that's a bad sign."

"Maybe we should just go," Christy said, looking back at me.

"Maybe we should, but I agree with Joel. We need a break. We've been on the run for weeks and I'd like to catch up on some sleep," I said.

Christy smiled tightly and went back to staring at the woods.

I put my back to the wall and took a minute to enjoy the afternoon sun. Frosty drifted over and put her head in my lap, so I closed my eyes and dozed for a while, content to enjoy a little quiet and companionship from the dog.

08:35 hours Approximate Location: Just outside of Oceanside

Voices from the front of the house woke me.

I shook away the cobwebs and found that Christy and Frosty had left me. They'd left me to be devoured if a zombie wandered across my form.

I rose and entered through the backdoor. No one was in the kitchen. Thanks a lot. With friends like these, who needed the zombie fucking apocalypse? I found them in the living room. Anna had her hand on her piece. Joel stood in front of the door and Roz had her back to the wall so she could cover the bay window. Christy hovered in the back of the room, looking like she wanted to bolt.

"Let me guess, more Zs. Jesus, why'd you guys leave me out there to get devoured?" I called.

The kitchen was deserted, and that just added to the realization that my friends had left me alone.

Then Christy's head appeared around the corner. She looked at me with large eyes. "Jackson, someone's here," she whispered.

"Someone like a live person? Or someone like a dude drooling blood and looking for a free lunch?" I asked as I walked into the living room. "Can't believe you all left me outside and asleep. What if a Z…"

Joel shot me a flat look.

"We just heard this guy, jeez, Jackson. You were only alone for a few seconds," Christy said.

"Guard the back door, man. Something's up with this fool," Joel said.

"I was just back there and there's no one out there."

"Dude. This guy might be a decoy while others move on our six. Grab a big gun and get ready for the worst."

I nodded and complied. If Joel was right, we needed to keep all entry points covered.

Joel moved his AR to the high ready position and covered the front door while Anna slid around a corner. If someone came in blasting, they had the entryway covered from two positions.

"Come on, Jackson," Roz said, moving into the kitchen.

She drew her gun and double-checked the magazine. Roz was armed with one of the 9mms-- the Sig, if I wasn't wrong.

I unholstered my Springfield XDM and followed her.

We dropped next to windows facing the backyard and peered outside.

"Hey man, I don't mean any harm," a man's voice called from outside. "Can you spare some food? Just a little bit, I got a wife and three kids. Please. We're all starving."

Joel didn't answer.

"I know you see me and I know you're there. There's at least four of you. I swear I don't want any trouble, just a little food. Anything you can spare. I've even got a few things I can share."

"Does he look dangerous?" I called from the kitchen.

"He looks like he's scared, but he also looks like he's wearing something under his shirt. My guess would be some kind of body armor. I can't see any weapons, but he hasn't turned either. Could be he's packing," Joel called back, just loud enough for us to hear him.

"Be careful," Roz said.

"Go away, man. I'm sorry to hear about your family but we don't have any extra food," Joel yelled.

"Please, just a few bites. We haven't had anything in days."

"We're well-armed, so just fuck off, okay? Go to town and raid just like the rest of us been doing," Joel tried to reason—like a Marine.

"You see anything?" I asked Roz.

"Nothing, but stay frosty."

The mutt heard her name and wandered over to see what we were up to. Frosty's wet nose on the back of my neck almost scared me out of my own skin.

I reached around and pulled her close. Frosty took a seat next to me and panted. The dog must have sensed our tension, because she cocked her head and stared in the direction of the door.

"What?" I asked her, like she could answer.

Frosty's ears perked up.

"Just give us a little bit and we'll leave you alone," the guy outside the house called.

"We? I thought it was just you," Joel called back.

"Shit," Roz said. "This guy's full of it."

Frosty stood and moved to the door. She bared

her teeth growled deep in her throat.

"Make this easy on yourself, man. You're going to give up some food one way or another."

"He's moving," Joel called. "I'm going to drop him."

Joel's AR spoke in the house. Glass tinkled as he fired a couple of rounds.

Frosty got spooked by the gunfire and prowled around the living room before she went to Christy and sat next to her.

"You get him?" I called.

"He's behind a car. As soon as he shows his skull I'm putting one in it."

"I don't like this, Joel."

"Keep it together, Jackson," Roz said.

"Movement, there." I pointed toward the East. Someone was fucking around by some shrubs.

I caught a glimpse of something dark, but then it was gone.

"I didn't see it," Roz said. "Wait, I see something but it's at three o'clock."

"Someone's trying to flank us," I called to Joel.

"Then put them the fuck down," he said.

I pushed the window up and it gave without a screech--thank goodness for the new house. All I needed was for it to give us away.

I lifted my pistol and aimed where I'd seen the shadow, but it didn't reappear.

"I got the other side, Jackson. You start shooting and be sure to call out targets. I'll do the same," Roz said.

Over the weeks we'd come under fire from a variety of bad guys. One thing I'd learned early on was that I'd rather face a horde of ravenous Zs than a bunch of dudes with guns. The mercenaries we'd been holed up with had shown me just how fast you could go down if someone had you in their sights. Now I felt like that again, like I was in the crosshairs.

A gun rang out and something struck the door. I dropped to all fours.

"Dumbass can't hit the side of a barn," Roz said.

She raised her head high enough to peek over the windowsill, then lowered herself back down.

Joel fired from the front of the house.

Frosty was smart and moved away from the door. She ran into the living room, hopefully to sit with Christy in a quiet corner. If someone got us and came through the door, they'd be in for a surprise when the dog took them down and Christy opened fire.

I took a quick look and saw a person moving across the line of shrubs near the woods. I poked my gun out the window and aimed, leading the target as it moved. I exhaled and squeezed the trigger. The gun bucked in my hand and the figure dropped to the ground, so I followed up with a couple more shots.

"I think I got him," I turned and said to Roz.

A bullet burst through the window overhead and made me kiss the floor.

"I don't think you got him," Roz said.

She lifted herself off the ground and aimed. She took a couple of seconds to zero in and fired a pair of rounds.

"I saw three of them back there but they don't look well-armed. Handguns, most likely," Roz said. "Hope one of them isn't toting a shotgun. I'd kill to have my Remington again."

I took a look, but no one moved back there.

"I'll cover from upstairs," Anna said, then she pounded up the stairs.

"Watch the backyard, Sails. I think a couple got around the house. I got this asshole," Joel said.

"Aye," she called.

Something rattled on the side of the house. I strained to see over the windowsill, but there was no way to spot them without opening the back door.

"I think they're trying to get into the camper," Roz said.

"Goddamn it. I'm going out there," Joel said.

"Joel, wait. We don't know how many there are. You might be walking into a trap," I said.

"That's why you're going to come up here and cover me. Roz, you got the back, Sails has the high ground, Jackson will cover me," he said.

I shook my head and moved into the living room. Christy was huddled up with Frosty, but she looked very determined. She held her revolver in a shaky hand, but I was pretty sure the kid would drop anyone who came through the door.

"Creed, lay down a few rounds near that burned-up Mustang. I got him bottled up. If he peeks out, pop him. Stay in the doorway, behind the wall, and make sure he doesn't shoot me in the back," Joel said, and put his hand on the doorknob.

"Dude, I don't know if I can do this," I said.

"Piece of cake, brother, just aim and shoot. That guy's probably more scared than you since I've been putting some heavy ammo on him. In a few minutes, all of these assholes are going to wish they'd stayed the hell away," Joel said.

I nodded and sucked in a few breaths. I took station at the bay window and sighted the car. No shape had presented itself yet.

Joel opened the door and dropped to his knees. His gun swept up to the ready as he studied the battlefield.

"When I move, pop two rounds at the car. I think he's behind the hood. Just spook him until I'm out of sight."

A gun spoke from upstairs--Anna's big .357, if I wasn't mistaken.

Joel moved, so I did as he'd instructed. I fired a round, and then another one. Both struck the top of the car.

The figure that had been hiding dove from cover and sprinted toward a house. I aimed, exhaled, and dropped him with a single round. His arms flew up and he fell face first into the unfinished lawn across the street. He didn't move again.

Joel was already gone, so I moved to the door to cover his exit.

#

08:35 hours Approximate
Location: Just outside of Oceanside

Anna's gun boomed again from upstairs. Then Roz opened fire. I held my handgun nice and high, ready to shoot anything else that twitched. I tried hard not to think about the man I'd just killed.

Jesus, but it had been him or us, and he hadn't exactly wanted to sit around and sing campfire songs. This guy could have been a Reaver and wanted to kill us and take our supplies. Worse, what if he'd got ahold of Christy? I didn't want to contemplate what crazy men might have done to her.

Joel fired a half dozen times. I ignored his advice and moved out onto the porch so I could see what he was firing at, but his form had disappeared. I backed up and kept myself in the little bit of shadow the roof provided.

Anna fired again.

"One down," she called.

I studied the street, gun raised, looking for targets. The only thing that stood out was the body of the bad guy I'd taken out. I drifted to the other side of the unfinished porch and kept a lookout.

I glanced over my shoulder repeatedly as I

waited for one of the attackers to come back.

Joel's gun sounded a few more times.

"Another one down. Anyone left back there, just throw your gun out and run," Joel said.

Someone returned fire.

Roz shot back and there was a scream.

I decided that I'd had enough sitting there, and hopped down off the porch. Then I hit the fucking ground as something exploded near my head and took a chunk of wood out of where I'd just been crouching. Had I not moved, I'd probably be dead.

A shape ran from the back yard. I managed to lift my gun and fire once. The man spun to the side and dropped his gun. It clattered across the sidewalk.

More shots from outside, and rounds kicked up dirt near the fleeing man. He tucked his head and ran toward me, but hugged the side of the house.

I dropped to my belly hard enough to knock the wind out of me. The shot I'd gotten off had been nothing but luck. As the man came alongside me, ten feet away, I managed to struggle to my knees. He froze in place and lifted his hands in the air. One of them dripped blood from where I'd hit him.

"Please, man. I didn't even want to go, but they told me I had to or they'd kick me out," he said.

The man turned out to be a kid, no more than eighteen or nineteen. He had a scraggly beard that looked more like a bunch of pubes. Tears streamed down his face as he moved past me.

"Clear up," Anna called.

"Clear down," Joel said from the other side of the house.

"Please, just let me go. I swear you'll never see me again," the kid said. "It's bad out there and we didn't have a choice. You'd do the same thing, right?"

"Wrong," I said and shot him.

He looked surprised for a split second as a red hole appeared above his eyes. He fell back in a heap and didn't move.

I exhaled and put my back against the wall. The shakes kicked in, and that was how Joel found me.

#

08:35 hours Approximate Location: Just outside of Oceanside

"Do I even need to say it?" Joel asked me later.

We'd dragged the bodies from the back of the house and placed them side by side in the front yard.

"I know, it was them or us."

"You did the right thing. For all we know the kid might have gone back for reinforcements and then burned us out."

"What makes you think there aren't more of them waiting to move on us?"

"I don't know, but we're entrenched now. I thought we could stay here a few days, but I think we need to get the fuck out of here in a few hours. We should rest up after we move the bodies," Joel said.

"Why move the bodies? There are enough corpses around as it is."

"Don't want someone seeing fresh dead and wondering what went down here," Joel said.

"Yeah, no sense in telling more raiders to keep away."

"I was thinking of shufflers," Joel said. "We don't want them to wonder if this is a house ripe for the picking."

"You make a lot of sense. Let's get them into another house," I said.

We tossed their backpacks into the middle of the yard. Joel and I went through pockets, but there wasn't much to find. A pocketknife, some coins; one guy had a wallet with a few dollars inside. He even had pictures of a family, but he wasn't in any of them. For all we knew, he might have lifted the wallet from someone else.

We came up with a few guns, including a .45 without any ammo. The man I'd shot across the street hadn't returned fire because he was out of rounds. The kid had even less on him, but we found two fifty-round boxes of 9mm in a backpack. Christy took the ammo and added it to our stash.

Roz and Anna kept watch while we took the bodies and dragged them into the house. Joel had torn off part of the tarp that was used to cover the truck. We rolled each body onto the heavy plastic, dragged them up the stairs, and tossed them in the living room. The house was much like ours: unfinished, with rolls of carpet, siding, and paint left in neat rows along the walls.

Once we had put the five in a row, Joel and I did the dirty work and put a knife through each skull except for the kid I'd shot. The bullet hole above his eyes stared back at me rudely.

They were dead, but was it possible they'd rise if they'd been bitten by Zs? None of us wanted to find out.

"Remember that TV show about zombies?" I asked.

"Yeah, I never saw it," Joel said.

"It was all drama and zombie killing. I guess they got that part right."

"I never cared for all that shit. Give me a good Bruce Willis or Danny Glover action flick over some weekly drama about emotions and monsters of the week. I like it when bullets are flying," Joel replied.

"I'm getting too old for this shit," I said, and planted the knife in a dead guy's eyeball. It stuck, and I had to hold his face to pull the blade out. I half-expected the dude to open his good eye, unhinge his mouth, and bite off part of my hand, but he was well and truly dead.

Joel snorted. "Welcome to the party, pal."

His blade went in and out of a head a lot easier than mine.

146

"There's going to be a lot more of this, isn't there?"

"As supplies dwindle and the Zs increase, yeah, there's always going to be a bad guy looking to take what's ours. We need to always be vigilant."

"Goddamn shame. The death of humanity bringing out the worst in people. Wonder how long until someone gets the drop on us?" I thought out loud.

"Ain't no one taking us out unless we let 'em," Joel said.

"Right, because we're badass action heroes," I said.

"No, because I'm a Marine and we're a fighting unit. Look at these assholes. Five of them and none of us got hit. I like those odds."

"I guess I did alright," I said.

"Yeah you did, you dumb squid, but don't get cocky," Joel said.

"Sure, Han Solo. I'll keep that in mind," I said.

Joel chuckled.

We slit the plastic covering and ripped it off a roll of carpet. Joel and I rolled it out and used it to cover the dead. As far as burials went it wasn't the best, but at least these guys were going to hell covered in light blue carpeting.

The rest of the evening was less eventful. We ate, played cards, and tried not to talk about the battle. I wanted to run for the hills, but Joel argued that we'd be better off after a night of sleep. I didn't draw first watch, and for a wonder, I was asleep in five minutes.

03:35 hours Approximate Location: Just outside of Oceanside

"Creed," a shuffler whispered in my ear.

I shot up and reached for my wrench with one hand; my other reached out to grab anything else I could get ahold of. I'd been dreaming of mountains of chocolate and ice cream, in that order. Then a Z rose out of the mess and I was stumbling back, and that was how I came awake.

Joel grabbed my wrist before I could swing my fist into his face. He was wiry but strong, I'll give him that. My heart pounded in my chest as I fought back panic.

"The fuck, man?" I said.

"Keep it down. We got company," Joel said, sounding like he was in an action movie.

"Like dinner company, or fucking Zs?"

"Dinner. They want to eat us."

I shook my head to clear away the fog, and wished I had about a gallon of coffee to slug back.

"Shit. Where?"

"Movement all around out there. It's goddamn eerie, man," Joel whispered.

Anna was on her feet and checking her weapons. Christy held onto Frosty and alternated between stroking her head and holding her mouth to show her that we needed silence. Roz sat next to a window and peered into the darkness. She'd moved the corner of our improvised carpet-curtain up so she had a viewport.

"Zs are eerie."

"They are, but these guys are being quiet. It's like they know we're here. I haven't seen anything like it before," Joel said.

Anna moved next to us and dropped to a crouch. "I count five or six near the back and another dozen at the front. They're standing around staring at the house."

"We're trapped," Joel said.

"Hold the fuck up," I said, finally shaking sleepiness from my head. "Are you saying they're out there waiting for us? Like they *planned* this?"

"Pretty much," Roz said as she joined us.

"We need to get the fuck out of this place and fast. Frontal assault. We go out shooting, get in the truck, and haul ass."

"There's more in the back. I saw them hanging around the outskirts of the yard," Roz said. "It's murky, so I couldn't see them very well."

Joel dug around in his backpack and came up with his old NVGs. He unwrapped them and pushed buttons, and slid them over his head.

"Batteries low. I'll do a fast sweep from inside. Stay here," he said and slipped the goggles over his head.

Joel left the kitchen and moved out. He stopped at a window facing into the backyard and stared.

We'd left most of our weapons out, having done an ammo check earlier. We'd depleted the majority of our rounds escaping the last few encounters. The few boxes I'd picked up from the old woman in town helped, but mainly Joel, since they were for his assault rifle.

Anna dug out a small stash of .357 rounds and she dumped a handful into her pocket. With an 8-round cylinder, she would be able to reload at least one more time.

Roz went over her weapons while I tucked the Springfield XDM into my belt. The wrench was always at hand and never ran out of ammo. I was likely to run out of juice swinging the damn thing before my partners ran out of bullets.

Joel returned. He put a pair of large cans down, then slid the NVGs off and tucked them into his backpack.

"Damn. Probably thirty or forty out there. I lost count."

"What's that?" I asked, pointing at the cans.

"Paint thinner. Time to light up the night so we can get the hell out of here."

"What, Molotovs?"

"Yep," Joel replied. "We don't have cans and bottles, so we'll improvise. Gather up the empty cans and fill them about halfway. Jam a piece of wadded up cloth inside so it's good and soaked. Be careful not to sop that shit all over the side. When we light 'em, you need a few seconds to throw."

"Is this going to work?" Roz asked.

"Better than sitting on our asses and waiting for them to wander away."

"Dude. How are we going to keep from getting burned? The thinner's gonna splash all over the place when we try to throw the stupid cans," I said. "Not to mention Frosty. If she sees fire she might freak the fuck out."

"Tape. Just a little over the top. Cover the can so the cloth hangs out, but not too tight. Frosty's too smart to run at the sight of fire. Dog's smarter than me," Joel said.

"She is a keeper," I said and rubbed her head.

We gathered half a dozen empty cans and put them near the back door. Roz ripped a shirt into big clumps while Joel poured.

"Why not wait?" Christy asked.

"What?" Joel said.

"Just wait. They're dumb Zs, so they'll wander off soon."

Joel scratched his head.

"She's right. Stay inside, chill. Wait," I said.

More than anything I wanted to lay down and sleep for a few more hours. I rubbed grit out of my eyes and looked at my sleeping mat.

"No. We need to get the fuck out of here. Something is up. I didn't see a shuffler, but something weird is happening. Zs don't just hang around in clumps like that."

Something hit the front door hard enough to

shake the side of the house. We went still and waited, wide eyes staring at each other.

The door shook again.

"Right. Plan A: get-the-fuck-out sounds like a winner to me," I said.

"You got that right, man. We get trapped in here and we're screwed, so as they say in your branch of the military, all hands on deck," Joel said.

"You heard the Sarge," I said, trying to sound badass.

"I'll crack a window and throw the first can. That should give us enough light to see what we're up against. After that, we move to the truck. Push any slow fuckers to the ground. Don't stand around trying to kill them all. We're interested in speed, people." Joel looked around our small party.

I nodded and lifted my wrench.

We assembled by the back door with gear stowed back in our packs. We'd have to leave some stuff behind, but I tossed out a few clothes and gave up my sleeping mat in favor of jamming all of our food supplies into my backpack.

Joel held his hand up for silence. I looked outside, but the moon was obscured by clouds, so making out Zs was practically impossible.

Something hit the roof. Then it happened again. A window shattered, and the sound of feet upstairs made my hair stand on end. Then more crashes, like the house was being broken into by a giant hammer.

"Fucking shufflers," I said.

"Don't waste ammo," Joel whispered. "When I start shooting, you all start tossing bombs at anything moving around back there. Move fast to the truck and get it started. Don't stop to kill. Like I said, speed is your friend."

"Is that really the best plan? To have a bunch of burning Zs running around out there?"

"It'll provide enough light to get out. Just don't let one of the flamers take you down," Joel said.

"This shit isn't going to work," Roz said.

"Better idea?" Joel asked.

"I got nothing," I said.

Roz just shook her head.

Joel slipped a pair of loaded mags into his kit and moved toward the stairs.

"Joel, what are you going to do?"

"What I do best, muthafucka. Shoot the bad guys."

Then he was gone.

TIMOTHY W. LONG

Overrun

03:30 hours approximate
Location: Just outside of Oceanside

Joel's departing form wasn't what I wanted to see. With his skills--not to mention his assault rifle--it was going to be up to us to secure the area and make it to the truck in one piece. There were only about fifty feet separating us from freedom, but it might as well have been fifty miles.

Our weapons were piled next to the window, so I grabbed the little hell-raiser we'd dug up in the abandoned house a few days ago. The Sig home defense assault rifle was loaded and ready for action. I had a spare mag filled with .45 ammo, so I shoved it into my pocket.

My backup was the Springfield XDM 9mm. I had one extra magazine, but it was only half-full — I guess I'm still an optimist after all this shit. I pulled it out of the holster, slipped the magazine out and made sure it was filled. After slamming it home, I racked back the slide and let it slam shut, loading a fresh round into the breach.

I didn't want to fight these things. I wanted to follow Joel's advice and make a run for it. At the same time I felt a sense of panic, because he was stuck in the house fighting shufflers without backup. As if to punctuate my thoughts, his rifle hammered away from upstairs a couple of times before going quiet. The ceiling creaked as figures moved around upstairs.

Frosty was on her feet and growling toward the back door. I patted her head and tried to reassure her.

Roz kept her cool, even if she did keep looking over her shoulder toward the stairs. No doubt she wanted to go as backup. She grabbed my upper arm and gave me a squeeze. I nodded to her, hoping she got my intention, which was to say "we got this". I didn't actually feel like we had anything but a slow death in our near future.

The ceiling rattled as things up there moved. Joel's gun sounded a couple of times, and one particularly loud crash probably meant something had just bit the dust. I hoped it wasn't my buddy.

Moans from the outside drew my attention to the window.

"Light me," Roz said.

Anna put a lighter to the flammable rag and it flared to life. Roz didn't waste any time and threw, but it fell short and splattered paint thinner a few feet short of the Zs. The yard lit up in a spooky glow, making the shadowy figures that approached look more like demons than the undead. I tried to count them, but gave up at twelve.

"Should we go?" asked Christy.

She knelt next to me, the snub-nosed .38 in one hand. She'd picked up a copper water pipe from somewhere in the house, and held it in her other hand. Christy's eyes were wide and nervous.

"We need more light," I said. "Christy, when we move, don't let go of Frosty if you can help it. She's gonna go batshit and we need to get her into the truck in one piece."

"Sorry about my short throw. I thought that stuff was going to splash all over my hand," Roz said.

I thought the same thing as I hefted one of the cans. It wasn't quite half-full, and the smell made me blink my eyes a couple of times. Anna held up the lighter.

The shufflers upstairs made a hell of a racket. Joel's gun spoke a couple of times, and something hit the floor above hard enough to shake the glass light fixture. Then it was quiet.

Frosty wasn't too happy with all the noise. Her hackles rose and she bared her teeth. She alternated between growling in the direction Joel had disappeared and toward the noise in the front yard.

I moved next, and Roz slid out of the way. I wanted to throw right-handed, but was sure the damn thing was going to blaze up and burn my hand. We didn't have time to make these things very well. My can had held some of the stew we'd enjoyed the night before, and now it sloshed with flammable liquid.

The ceiling shook again under pounding feet. Joel's gun fired several times and then it was quiet again.

Anna lit the cloth. The fire flared immediately and just like Roz, I panicked and threw. The night came alive with more light, but I'd hit nothing.

"Oh Jesus," Anna exclaimed.

Anna picked up a can and shouldered me aside. She still cradled her injured arm, but managed to do a hell of a lot better than me or Roz. As soon as the cloth was lit, she held the can tilted slightly until she was sure it was aflame. Throwing from her fingertips, the can sailed through the air and plastered a Z in the chest.

Thinner exploded all over the man. He howled and fell back, knocking down another Z. The pair thrashed, and managed to make the flames even worse.

Joel pounded into the kitchen and nearly got a face full of wrench.

"*Dude.*"

"Gimme a can. I'm gonna light this place up. I took down a shuffler, injured another one, but one other fucker is still sneaking around up there, too scared to show his face. See how he likes *this* shit."

Joel snagged a can and Roz lit the rag. He moved fast, with the mini-torch lighting his way.

A few seconds later there was a *whoosh* and something screamed: a tiny *whoof* of noise as the improvised bomb must have come to life.

Frosty nearly broke free. I grabbed her collar, and tried to reassure her with a few soft words.

"We're out of here," I said and grabbed another can. "Christy, take the lighter and fire us up as we go. Follow and get ready to pop anything that gets too close."

She nodded.

Roz, Anna, and I each took one of the last three improvised Molotovs. I pushed the back door open and was on the landing before I could acknowledge the fact that I was holding a can of flame that could light me up just as quickly as it could a Z. With the backyard now illuminated, it was easier to make out the Zs. I drew back and let the can sail. It splashed across a Z and turned it into a walking torch.

I had other issues.

In my excitement I'd managed to splash flammable liquid over my hand and shirt. When I threw I knew I was in trouble.

Flames roared to life on the Z's shirt. It stumbled back into another creeper and set his ass on fire. They actually looked like they were scared of the flames as they tripped, and ran into each other.

I flailed my arm around as fire and pain raced across the top of my hand.

Anna slapped at my burning appendage while

Roz moved into position, lit her can, and tossed it.

As far as Molotovs went, I'd have to say these weren't the best idea. With the partially-exposed lids, a lot of fluid leaked out as they were jostled. Flames followed on a stream of paint thinner, further lighting the night, but also splashing fire over the partially-finished yard.

Zs by the dozens moved in on our position. They stumbled, flailed, shambled, and generally scared the ever-living *fuck* out of me. I moved in front of Anna as I slapped my hand into my armpit to extinguish the blaze.

"Move!" Anna said, and gave me a small push.

I did.

With the wrench in my off hand, I took the two steps to the yard and smashed a Z to the ground. Dude was reaching for me, his shirt on fire, flames eating at his face. His mouth was a horror of broken teeth, dried, copper-tinged blood, and something that might have been a nose. White and partially-desiccated eyes fixed on mine.

I hit him hard enough to cave in the side of his head. He dropped, but his body caught my legs, and I staggered into Anna.

Roz came to the rescue and shot a flailer between the eyes. The Z's head snapped back, and her body hit the ground.

They were all around us.

Frosty darted in and nipped at a Z, then danced around as it reached for her. The dog played it smart and kept out of the rotter's grasp.

Christy called to Frosty, so the dog shot between the legs of a Z, knocking it down.

In a panic I recovered, and did a little half-spin as I tried to decide which of the creepy crawlers to take on first.

There was a teenage kid who was taller than me and skinny as a rail. His clothes were rags, his once grey-and-black camo shorts barely hanging onto his hips. An older couple dressed in the remains of hospital smocks. The woman still trailed an IV tube from one arm. The man wore a cast that immobilized his leg, but he shuffle-stepped like he was in a weird dance.

I shoved the couple aside, batted the kid's hands away with my wrench and kicked him into a flaming Z who shambled in circles.

Anna drew her big handgun and shot the kid as he sat up and reached for me.

Christy shot the woman with the IV and clipped the side of her neck. I swung up and caught her under her chin. Rotted teeth flew, and part of her head broke loose. The Z flew backward into another of the rotted things, and the pair fell in a heap.

With our way free and only a dozen or so feet from us to the truck, I thought we now had a straight shot.

Hands reached for me, so I slapped them aside.

Frosty barked at something, but I didn't have time to look.

I made out the truck in the murk and ran

straight for it. I had the whole thing mapped out in my head. I'd beat down the Z that was in front of me. Reach the truck, make myself a big barricade while the others got to my location. They'd load and then we'd be inside. We'd be surrounded, but with any luck the big truck would shove the dead aside. That was, if the shufflers didn't hit us first.

I almost made it.

03:45 hours approximate
Location: Just outside of Oceanside

Sure enough, a shuffler dropped from the roof and hit me from behind.

He was a snarling mess of wounds and open sores. His eyes glowed with hate and his mouth opened to reveal teeth filed to points. The smell was the worst: like someone had left a body covered in dead fish to rot in the sun.

He caught my leg and I nearly fell, but stumbled into the truck and recovered.

I gagged as I turned to confront him.

A Z had been closing in on me, but I had his number and kicked back, catching him in the groin. The decomposing little shit bent at the waist and collapsed.

The shuffler moved sinuous as a whip, and swung out a leg to catch Anna. She stumbled back and caught herself on the porch railing. Roz reached for her, but the shuffler spun and took her to the ground. She thrashed as it covered her and leaned in to rip at her face. I ignored a Z that almost got a hand on me, and rushed in.

I grabbed the rotting creature by a foot and with adrenaline roaring in my ears, ripped it off of Roz. The shuffler wasn't much more than flesh and bone, but it was strong and lashed a foot up, catching me in the shoulder.

My left arm went numb, but I didn't let go. I got my other hand on its ankle and used all of my strength to rip the bastard off of Roz and fling it at another Z. The shuffler didn't even hesitate; it scrambled to all fours and leapt.

Roz clambered back, legs kicking at the ground as she tried to get to the porch.

Anna lifted her gun and fired, but the shuffler was fast, and the shot whizzed past its head.

Frosty darted between Zs in the yard, avoiding the burning Zs, but harrying others.

The night took on a glow as flames rushed across the upper story.

In the wan light, I caught a female Z coming at me. I didn't want to take my eyes off Roz and the shuffler, but I couldn't ignore the arm that looped over my neck. Teeth went for my shoulder, so I whipped my elbow around and caught her in the side of the head.

Roz fell under the smart Z again. I howled in fury as I shook off the rotting Z and lifted my wrench, intent on cracking shuffler bones.

Roz got her handgun up to shoot the Z, but it

batted her firearm aside.

Anna tried to get a good shot, but it was obvious that if she fired, she had every chance of hitting Roz as well.

I hit the shuffler's leg, and bones cracked. It hissed in fury, and its head spun to regard me. Eyes glowed with malevolent intelligence as they swept over me. It rose up and lashed at me with one claw-like hand. I drew back and turned so he didn't have a chance at my numb shoulder. Make that *kind of* numb. Feeling was returning, and it hurt like a bitch.

A Z was on me. I didn't have time for this Mickey Mouse bullshit, so I lifted my wrench and took off most of its head.

Anna drew her knife and slashed at the shuffler from behind. She tried to drive the blade into his neck, but the creature was fast, and got a sliced shoulder for his efforts. Take that, you bastard.

Roz choked and rolled onto her side.

The shuffler turned to take on Anna, so I swept the wrench around and hit him in the arm. I'd aimed higher, but my shoulder wasn't exactly responding to what my brain tried to tell it to do. Anna lashed at the thing again as it came up on its two feet. Driving forward, she cut him hard enough to sever fingers.

The shuffler shrieked and leapt.

Anna shifted to the side but he still bowled her over. He scrambled over her as she fought him off.

"No!" I screamed, and got hit by another Z as I

moved to help.

Frosty grabbed the shuffler's pant leg and pulled. The bastard struck back, and Frosty whimpered as her snout took the blow. She backed up and shook her head. Christy grabbed Frosty's collar and tugged the dog away from the melee.

Joel appeared in the doorway. I caught sight of him out of the corner of my eye. He paused on the landing, lifted his gun, and calmly dropped a pair of Zs that were bearing down on me.

Anna was my priority. If not for him the two Zs probably would have taken me to the ground. Leave it to Joel Fucking Kelly to come to the rescue.

Anna kicked at the Z as it crawled over her.

Roz rolled onto her back, saw the shuffler as it attacked Anna, and didn't sit around waiting for help. She scissor-kicked from her side and caught the rotter in the thigh. A normal man would have howled with pain, but this just pissed off the shuffler.

"Fuck you, asshole," she said and kicked again.

The shuffler shrugged off the blows, and his mouth leapt at Anna.

Anna did a neat trick where she leveraged her body off the ground and twisted to dump the shuffler on his side. She tried to move away, but the thing scrambled to its knees and then went for her.

Christy dashed past Joel with a flaming can in one hand. She skipped the last step, hit the ground running, and only paused to slam the improvised Molotov onto the shuffler's head.

Anna crab-walked out of the way as fire streamed around them.

The shuffler screeched as his hair flared to life. He leapt off of Anna and fell, slapping at his head as the fire spread. Skin and stringy hair burned. The shuffler tried to bat at the fire, but as he came up into a kneeling position, Joel put an end to his struggles with a shot to the head. The 5.56 round passed through his skull and exited with an impressive amount of red and rotted brain matter.

The shuffler's head snapped back, and for a second he stared with hatred at us. Even *I* was fucking shocked at how long it took for the thing to slump to the side.

Joel and I helped the ladies to their feet, and he quickly took point. He kicked a Z out of the way and shot another at almost point-blank range, blowing half its head off in the process.

Anna limped, and warded her injured arm, holding it tight against her body. Her Smith & Wesson hung in her other hand. Roz clung to me, her arm draped around my waist. She stepped on something on the ground and almost fell. I lifted her back up, surprised at how weak she seemed.

Christy moved to my side, Frosty sticking close to her. Christy had her little snub-nosed revolver in hand and fired into the darkness. The round caught a shambling Z in the shoulder. He spun away and crashed into another rotting corpse, and the two went down in a heap of limbs.

Behind me, flames crept out of the second-story windows, casting an orange and yellow haze over the backyard. I didn't want to think about the things coming for us, but I looked anyway. I should have kept my damn eyes front and center, because there were more than enough to kill us.

"Joel, we're about to be overrun!"

"I know, fuck, we're here though. Get them in the back and I'll start the truck. Christy, shoot any fucker that gets close, and don't let Frosty run off. Get her in the front seat with you."

"Got it," she said. Christy opened the gun's cylinder and dropped spent shells on the lawn. With deft and practiced fingers, she reloaded from her jeans pocket.

I had to kick a Z out of the way. The shambler had been hanging out in the tiny space between the camper and the side of the house. He fell on his back, and when he looked up I met his gaze with a blow to the head. My wrench felt like a fifty-pound lead pipe, but I managed to lift it one more time.

Anna slid past me and hit the side of the truck. She peeked around the corner and held up a hand.

Joel hopped in the driver's seat and started the truck. In the movies this would be the part where the engine wouldn't turn over no matter how many times Joel cranked it. The first piece of good luck all night occurred when the engine roared to life.

Anna swung around the back of the truck and fired two measured shots.

"Clear!" she said.

Roz and I clutched at each other as Anna opened the back door. She watched our six as I helped Roz on board. I didn't need to be reminded that we were surrounded, so the Zs thumping at the sides and back of the truck were like hammer blows upside my now-aching head. I needed water, some aspirin, and about fifteen hours of fucking sleep.

Roz and I collapsed on the floor. Anna slammed the door shut and locked it. The truck's engine engaged and Joel backed up. Anna was thrown off her feet and hit the little dining table. She grabbed at the edge, but lost the battle and was tossed to the ground.

"Fuck *me*!" she said.

###

04:05 hours approximate
Location: Just outside of Oceanside

I struggled to get on my hands and knees as the truck rocked us. I managed to pull Roz to my chest when Joel hit the engine again. The truck accelerated while I struggled to get Roz to the bed. Her breathing was labored and she had gone almost completely limp in my hands.

"Come on Roz, we're just about out of here. Tell me what hurts, okay?" I said.

She shrugged and pointed at her mouth.

The interior of the camper was cold and dark, so Anna hit the overhead light.

I nearly dropped Roz.

Her mouth was covered in blood and gore. She struggled away from me, so I let her go.

Roz spit out a mass of blood and saliva, then furiously wiped at her mouth with her sleeve. She rolled to her side, curled up in a ball and vomited. The reek hit me and I almost threw up myself. That would have been an interesting chain reaction, because Anna might have joined the barf patrol.

"What's wrong with her?" Anna asked.

"Don't know," I said.

I stared at Roz in horror. If she'd been bitten, we needed to get rid of her, and soon. I liked Roz a lot. We'd even shared a moment in a garage a few months back. She'd been with us ever since. If we had to toss her, I didn't want to be the one to tell Joel.

The truck spun tires and swerved to the right, and I was thrown off my feet.

"Jesus, Joel!" I yelled.

I doubt Joel heard me, but the truck accelerated for a full twenty seconds before he slammed on the brakes again. This time I'd barely gotten to all fours when I face-planted onto the tile floor. My arm stretched out to stop my forward momentum, but my nose ended up taking the impact anyway.

Cursing, I pushed myself back up and got to

my feet. I wedged myself between the floor and the low ceiling and held on for dear life, because sure enough, the truck roared forward again. This time I got to the little table and sat down before Joel could knock me down again.

Roz was curled up in a ball and shaking. Anna lay next to her, and shot pleading looks my way.

"Can you tell what's going on with Roz? Was she bit?" I asked.

I rubbed at my nose and didn't find blood, but it hurt like hell.

"She's wounded, but I can't tell how it happened," Anna said. Her eyes didn't meet mine.

Anna's body language changed. She tensed and her hand crept to her holster.

"Is she?" I couldn't finish.

"I said I don't know."

"Roz. You okay?" I asked.

She nodded but didn't reply. One of her arms wrapped around her head like it was about to explode.

"Fuck," Anna said, which seemed to sum up what I was thinking as well.

That was all she got out before we hit something. *Two* somethings. The truck swerved again, and then came to a shuddering stop.

Frosty was in the front with Joel and Christy, but something must have spooked her, because her bark carried into the camper.

Roz rolled across the floor and hit the little bed. Anna and I managed to hang onto the table. The truck moved again and came to a halt.

"He's playing fucking pinball up there," I muttered.

I moved to the window and slid the curtain aside. Anna didn't move, and kept an eye on Roz.

"What's going on out there?" Anna said.

I didn't even have the words to answer her.

The quiet neighborhood we'd found eight hours ago was filled with the dead. They were in the streets, streaming around houses, shambling corpses covered in rags and filth. White eyes fixed on nothing as they advanced.

The truck backed up a half block and came to a halt again as we hit a couple of Zs. They bounced under the bed and were chewed up by tires.

"We are so fucked," I finally said.

Anna moved to the window and looked outside. She turned to me, her lips a slit as her mind churned.

"Maybe he can find a way out," Anna said.

Joel's assault rifle spoke. It rattled off a few measured shots, and then the truck moved once again. It accelerated and swerved to the right. Anna grabbed at me as I reached up and wedged myself against the roof.

Another shot rang out. From the sounds, it was the little revolver that Christy carried. I didn't stop to let the surrounding horror consume me. I needed to assess the threat from up high, and there was only one way to do that and communicate with Joel.

The trapdoor was small, but I thought I could at least get my head out, and maybe an arm.

"Keep an eye on her," I nodded at Roz.

I pushed a chair in the middle of the floor and stooped as I stepped on it. The hatch popped up, but there was a bar that kept it from opening all of the way. I hit the little door, but it was bolted tightly. I grabbed the bar that held it in place and twisted until it popped loose. The screw that held it against the opening wasn't that strong, and the head hit the floor. It popped like a champagne cork and flew off. With any luck, it smacked a Z upside the head.

I grabbed my 9mm and pushed myself up into the opening. I wiggled my gun hand out and got my upper body wedged in the entry. With a little more twisting I managed to get my shoulder in along with my arm, so I hoisted myself up and on top of the roof, which wanted to buckle under me.

It was still dark, but morning was coming on, and with it, enough light to wish it was still pitch black. The things were all around us, and I understood now why Joel had been bouncing us all over the damn place: the Zs were an ocean in every direction, illuminated by the burning house we'd left behind. Sure enough, Joel's idea had turned into an inferno. That meant it wouldn't take long for the rest of the neighborhood to go up in flames.

Something rattled loudly in the distance, shaking the night. I twisted around, looking for the source of the sound, pretty sure I knew what it emanated from.

Hands hit the side of the camper as they reached for me, but I was far enough up that they weren't a threat.

Christy's head appeared as she slid out of her window and crawled on top of the cab. She shot a Z that would have grabbed her ankle, and slithered on top of the truck.

"Joel said we have to get inside and fortify."

"How were you planning to get in here?" I asked.

"You were going to open the little roof door, duh," Christy rolled her eyes.

I shot a Z that got a little too adventurous. The bullet passed above one eye and exited the back of his head with a fair amount of dead brain matter.

Joel leaned out of the window and shot a pair of Zs in rapid succession. The bodies fell away into the crowd.

"SITREP?" Joel turned and shouted at me.

"One word: fucked!"

"That's three words. How fucked?"

"We are so fucked, dude," I yelled back.

Joel nodded and ducked back into the truck. "Coming out the starboard side."

"When you use fancy navy terms I get all hot in my pants, Joel," I called back. "What about Frosty?"

"I hope you got that smart mouth ready when they close in on us and start eating us feet first. I'm

173

going to leave her here for now until I come up with a better plan."

"A better plan? Better to let her go. Frosty's smart and quick. She'll get away," I said.

Gunfire again as he shot three or four Zs that were crowding around the passenger side window. Joel slithered out the side of the truck, and shot a Z in the process.

I leaned over and covered him, shooting a man with dreads. Dude's head snapped back, and he was a twice-dead dread. "Joel, don't, man. You won't make it."

Joel shot another Z. "New plan," he yelled.

Joel disappeared and the truck jarred me against the roof. I grabbed the hatch and held on with a death grip as he shifted into reverse. The way behind us wasn't much clearer, but I understood what he was doing even as the truck backed up. With the weight of the camper we'd have more traction. Couple that with the fact that it was rear drive, and we'd buy ourselves a few more minutes, at the very least.

Christy got creative and used the camper's small side window to haul herself up. A Z reached for her, but she was quick to kick him in the head. He fell back and quickly stretched for her again. Christy grasped the edge of the camper's roof. I pushed through the portal and stuck my hand out for her, but she slipped away.

A Z roared and I just about went over the side.

Christy's hand reappeared, and this time I put

a death grip on her wrist and pulled her up.

"Ouch, Creed. You're going to break my arm."

"I thought they got you, Christy, Jesus!" I said, and hugged her as I dragged her toward me.

She slithered around me and grabbed hold of the half-demolished hatch. I helped her turn around and got my arm around her waist.

"I'm going back in. You need to be right behind me, got it?"

She nodded, eyes wide.

I scrambled for purchase as we turned multiple Zs into speed bumps. The truck's rear lights lit up the faces of white-eyed ghouls before they were crushed to a pulp. Joel kept it at a steady fifteen or twenty miles an hour as he smashed the horde aside.

The hard part was getting my left arm back inside while I held onto Christy. She grasped the open hatch, slid around, and slipped her legs inside.

My feet hit the chair and I stumbled, falling the short distance, but managing to land with jarring impact.

"What in the fuck is going on out there?"

"It's bad, Anna."

Christy lowered her body into the camper. I got my hands around her and guided her to the floor.

"Roz?"

"Not any better, and all this goddamn bouncing around isn't helping. Do I need to go up there?" Anna asked.

"If you think it will help, sure."

Anna pushed me aside and stepped on the chair. It shifted beneath her, but she got her good arm up and pulled herself to her feet.

"Keep an eye on her," she said.

"I was kidding, I'll go back up there."

"Creed, I'm trained and I'm a better shot than you. Stay here and watch over Roz," she said, and then leaned close. "You know what to do if you have to."

"That's Roz," I whispered back.

"If she turns, she won't be anything except a danger. Do you really want a Z loose in the camper?"

Anna locked gazes with me, nodded once, and then climbed on the chair. She put her hand through the trapdoor and tugged her body into the spot I'd just occupied.

Anna's body didn't completely disappear from sight. She maneuvered around and got one hand inside the hatch. She pulled her gun and lay flat.

Christy dropped next to Roz to check on her. She'd taken a towel off the counter and used it to wipe Roz's face. The she grabbed a bottle of water and started to clean up the mess.

The truck came to a shuddering stop. I grabbed at the ceiling and managed to brace myself. Anna slid forward, but she quickly backed up until I could see her upper body again.

The truck moved forward, turned slightly, and then accelerated backward again. Hands pounded at the door, but the thumping of hands ceased after we moved, and was replaced by the thumping of bodies under the vehicle.

The truck once again slammed to a stop, and didn't move again. Anna shot until her big revolver ran dry, then handed it down to me.

"Where's the ammo?"

"In the pile. Just hand me another gun."

"How many Zs are there?" I asked.

"More than we have rounds for." She gave me a flat look.

Christy had already dug into our supply and come up with a compact Ruger .40 we'd acquired somewhere along the way. I shifted stuff around and found the little house sweeper.

"Coming up," I said and got on the chair again.

Anna shimmied over as I popped out of the hatch.

The night was lit up by the house we'd set on fire. Flames roared as the house was engulfed. The orange glow was genuinely creepy, with flares casting shadows over the undead.

To the North there was a road that looked clear. To the South lay an army of dead.

Between us and a shot at the road were at least a hundred shamblers. It's great to feel wanted, except when a bunch of people want to eat your flesh and blood.

"Joel." I pounded on the roof. "About a block and a half North of here, the road is free."

Joel yelled back an acknowledgment. His

assault rifle rattled a few times, clearing something of a path. He slowly backed the truck up, smooshing over bodies that reached for us even as he crushed them.

The truck roared ahead and I got my hand around Anna in case she lost her grip. She shimmied around so we had a good view of the front of the truck, and we both opened up, trying to drop as many of the Zs as possible.

The problem was that they just formed little speed bumps, but Joel wasn't deterred. He hit the high beams, bounced on a curb, tore over the sidewalk, and cut closely between two houses.

Our vehicle had enough blood and guts covering the hood and sides to make a horror movie fan stand up and shout for glee.

The yard was half-finished, and Joel had no choice but to drive over a couple of deep holes that had probably been dug for more trees. I got a glimpse of a Z rising out of one of the pits like a fresh-raised dead. The truck smacked him down and then bounced into the air. Anna hung onto me, and I held onto the hatch.

We were going to make it.

"Ow!" Christy called from inside.

"We see the road, Christy. Hang on."

What I'd taken for a low line of shrubs or trees turned out to have a different idea. As the truck bumped over the yard, the high beams told the tale: the road was indeed free, but Zs were closing in from every direction. Even this big-ass rig wouldn't be able to make it through that mess.

"I'll get us as far as I can," Joel called from inside the truck.

It was a great plan. Sadly, we didn't get very far.

I held on as Joel hit a fucking *wall* of zombies. Some were smashed aside, some were crushed underneath, and some exploded. Walking corpses, so I'd learned, tended to do that. Blood, guts, splattered brains, and body parts covered the front of the big truck, and with each impact, the body sustained more and more damage. There had to be a hundred of the things all around us, and instead of getting away from them, we came to a halt.

The truck died, and with it, the sound of the dead became the only thing I heard, until Anna took out a feisty, freshly-dead fuck who'd decided that he wanted to climb up the hood.

The engine turned over, caught with a weird noise that sounded like chains cracking together and then died again. Joel cranked a few more times, but the only answer was a grinding noise.

"Ah, shit!" he said.

I pushed myself up and shimmied through the little portal. My sides and arms felt like I'd been in a damn boxing ring with all of the scrapes and bruises.

Anna made room for me, but the roof bowed dangerously as we moved around.

Joel turned the key again and let it crank for a good ten seconds, but nothing happened, except the truck groaned like it had given up. *That's right, fuck you people who abused the shit out of me. I can only take so much.*

The dead closed in all around us.

"What do we do now?" Anna looked me in the eye and I saw something that I had rarely seen from her.

She was just as scared as me.

#

Uncertainty

05:20 hours approximate
Location: Just outside of Oceanside

Gunfire shattered the night.

The moans of the dead were the only noise that filled my ears. They also filled my soul with dread, because as many scrapes as we'd been in, this was the motherfucker that topped them all. Not for the first time we were completely surrounded, but this time I didn't have a plan, and judging by the defeated look on Joel's face, neither did he.

I'd been staring at the mass as they surrounded us, and my thoughts had turned to how we were all going to off each other. Would one of us shoot the rest? Would we sit around in a circle jerk and watch each other blow their brains out? Maybe we could just have Joel machine gun us into oblivion, and then he could do himself.

The funny thing was that I worried about my body after we were dead, so I had been looking around for things to set the camper on fire with.

Then my mind raced as I thought about

zombies eating our toasted bodies. Would they bring some Kansas City BBQ sauce to enjoy our ribs?

Joel managed to get out of the truck's window without being pulled into the mess of Zs. Anna and I had provided cover while he shimmied up the side and onto the roof, kicking away grasping hands in the process.

There'd been one real moment where I thought he was being dumb. Joel had grabbed a couple of boxes of ammo and flung them at us, then he'd ducked in for more after batting aside a couple of grabby assholes. What was the use of all that ammo when we were completely stuck? It would take a thousand rounds to get out of this mess.

The basis of a plan formed in my head. We'd take turns sitting on the camper shooting all of these bastards until we were out of bullets. If that happened, we'd have a chance.

Or until a couple of shufflers appeared.

The three of us shimmied into the camper.

"This ain't good," Joel said. "And what the hell is that fucking smell?"

"Roz got sick after we got her in here. Not like we can open a window and air the place out," I said. "We've been in worse spots than this, Joel."

"Nah, man. This is the worst. Thing is, the truck is stuck. I don't know if I got too much zombie shit in the grill or if we just hit a Z wall. All I know is I couldn't move forward or back. Engine died and I couldn't get it to restart."

"Wait it out," Anna said.

"I saw at least three shufflers out there. Glowing green eyes and everything. I can try to take them out, but hitting moving targets isn't as easy as it looks, and we got limited ammo," Joel said.

"So much for my plan," I muttered.

"What was it?" Joel asked.

"It was stupid. Next plan?"

"We don't have a choice. We have to wait it out, and maybe we can keep them out of the camper long enough so that they lose interest and wander away. All we have to do is shoot the shufflers," Anna said.

"Works for me," I nodded. "Put Joel and his assault rifle up there and he can pick off the fast ones."

"Good plan, but I'm almost out of rounds."

Joel moved to Roz's side and brushed the hair out of her face. His fist clenched when he saw the damage.

"She needs help," I muttered.

Hands pounded at the back door.

"I tried to clean up the wound, but there's a lot of blood and I didn't want to hurt her," Christy said.

"How could you let this happen?" Joel said.

I shook my head. What the *hell*? We didn't *let* anything happen; a shuffler had dropped on us and taken us by surprise. Anna had been the one to get the bastard off Roz while I fought my way back to them.

"It was so fast, Joel, you were there. Oh, wait, you went upstairs to kill stuff, remember, that's what you do."

"Fuck you, man. I saved your ass and you let her get attacked."

"Don't blame me. Coulda happened to any of us," I tried to reason.

"But it didn't, it happened to her."

Christy sat on the floor next to Roz and held a bloodied towel. Tears left a clean line through grime as they trickled down her face.

"Stop arguing," she said.

"We aren't arguing, because I'm right," Joel said.

He looked around the tiny cabin and I saw something in his eyes I'd never seen before: despair. He was at the end of his rope, and I wasn't going to be much help, because I felt the same way.

More hands beat at the trailer. The truck actually tilted as too many of them pushed.

"Joel, we can't argue about this right now. We need to deal with that," I nodded at the door.

Joel pointed at Roz. "*That* is a *real* problem. *That* is what we need to fix. Tired of watching your ass all the time."

The side of the cabin bowed in and the trailer lifted a half foot off the ground. I reached for the sink and caught myself.

"Calm down, man. You're just upset."

"I'm not going to be calm until we're out of this. We gotta get some help for Roz. Get back to the city and see if that crazy bitch with the meds has something that can fix her up."

"Dude, you sound like a crazy person," I said.

"Fuck you, Creed. The only thing crazy is that we're stuck in this shitty mess," Joel fumed. "I'm going to thin the herd. Better than sitting here waiting to die."

"So you're going to go sit up there and shoot until you're empty and maybe, just maybe, we'll be able to get to safety. Sounds like we're going to have to run. Did you plan to leave Roz here? Because it's going to take more than one of us to carry her."

"No one's getting left behind. Hand me some ammo," Joel said.

Christy was quick, gathering up a couple of magazines and handing them to Joel. He shoved a few in his pockets and handed over his empties.

"I don't think we have enough to fill them," Christy said.

"Do your best," Joel nodded.

"What about us? What do we do while you're up there saving us?" I asked.

"What *can* we do, man? What the fuck can we do? Roz's hurt, we're completely surrounded, and we can't just sit around with our thumbs up our asses. We don't even know if she's going to turn into one of those fucking things. Give me a better plan or get the hell out of the way."

Joel shouldered me aside and stepped on the chair. He pushed his assault rifle out of the portal and then wedged himself in.

"We need something better than shooting them, come on Joel. Let's think this through."

"Like I said," Joel yelled back. "Come up with a plan or sit down and shut the fuck up."

"Don't be an asshole, Joel. Roz needs you now, and so do Anna and Christy," I said, because I couldn't think of anything better to say.

Joel was pissed, yeah, but he wasn't thinking straight. Even if he had unlimited ammo, could he really clear this entire area, kill the shufflers, and then get us out of here? The chances were nil. Fucking *nil*, and he knew it.

Joel dropped back into the cabin and got in my face.

"What do you have in mind, smartass?" Joel waited.

"Not having a fucking pity party, that's one plan. You want to go up there and waste all of our ammo, be my guest, but then what?"

The camper bowed in on both sides.

"Then we get the truck unstuck and get the hell out of here. Thin the herd, because it's worked before, so man up or sit down here and cry like a bitch," Joel said.

"Shut up," I said.

"Don't tell me the fuck to…"

"They're listening to us argue. Just shut up," I whispered.

Joel stared daggers but nodded. We stood in silence as the moans rose around us.

#

We gave it a few minutes and sure enough, the pounding at the camper died down a little bit. Joel and I sat on opposite sides, him with one arm crossed around his AR-15 and the other on Roz's shoulder, me holding my wrench and wishing I was out there swinging it, because I was fucking mad as hell.

Joel had every right to be a pain in the ass and he had every right to be angry at our situation, but taking it out on me was the wrong move. We'd seen a lot of shit, but I'd never seen him this close to losing it.

If we lost Joel, where would we all be? I'd like to say that the girls and I would be fine and dandy and live to fight another day. After all, Anna Sails was badass enough for both of us. The fact that she was a woman and smaller than me meant that I'd initially discounted her as needing to be protected. Turned out she was more than up for the challenge, and had been the one to protect me on many occasions.

Christy had latched onto us, me in particular, and I'd done my best to teach her everything I knew about surviving the zombie fucking apocalypse. She was good with a gun, but sometimes rattled easily. That was understandable, because she was a kid, but I'd seen her step up on more than one occasion.

Then there was Roz. She was always steady. When we'd met her she'd been outside of her house and intent on shooting her dad, who had already become a Z. Since then she and Joel had bonded. Now there was something wrong with her. The shuffler had done some damage, and unlike a zombie's bite, it wasn't turning her. But what did that mean?

After Roz had finished puking her guts out, Christy had been nice enough to slop the mess into a corner and out of the way, but the smell wasn't any better.

Frosty barked from the front of the truck, then quieted down.

Some of the Zs continued to pound on the walls, but some had given up and wandered off-- or so I hoped. In an ideal world they'd all be gone, coast clear. As far as I was concerned, we needed to just stay put and hope the bastards found another bunch of people to terrorize.

It was another ten minutes before Joel decided he'd had enough. He rose to his feet and moved to the center of the camper, but didn't meet my eye. He looked back at Roz and then climbed onto the chair.

"Wait, Joel," I whispered.

He ignored me and pushed his head out of the

portal.

"Shit," he said when he dropped back down.

"Told you to wait," I said.

"Wouldn't matter. Damn Zs are just hanging around out there like they know we're still here. I'm gonna go see if the engine will turn over. Maybe it's cooled…" He didn't finish his sentence, because something hit the camper hard enough to make it shake.

Green eyes peered in from the entryway, and another pair appeared at the back door. I drew and shot before I'd thought it through. The sound of the 9mm in the tiny space was deafening, like I'd shoved cotton in my ears because a giant monkey playing cymbals had pounded my head.

Something hit the roof and Joel swung his assault rifle up. He dropped to one knee and aimed at the portal. When part of the ceiling buckled, he fired two rounds. There was a screech of pain, and then the roof buckled in another place.

I met the eyes of my companions and saw nothing but fear.

05:50 hours approximate
Location: Just outside of Oceanside

The pounding began in earnest. Fists hammered the truck and hands clawed at the windows.

The back of the camper flexed under the

pressure. Joel pushed back.

A side window shattered and Zs reached inside. Anna pulled her knife and slashed at the hands that hunted for our flesh. A finger hit the ground and one of the Zs withdrew, but more hands appeared in its place.

I stood up and lifted my wrench. When they came through, I was going to be a wall capable of swinging heavy steel. I'd bash in every head I could reach before they took me down.

A blast from outside the camper scared the shit out of me.

Another blast and one of the creatures on top of the vehicle fell off with a thump. Several more gunshots, and the things above us departed. Joel and I looked at each other but he was the first one to say it. "Hit the deck!"

I got on my belly and hoped whoever was out there didn't spray our vehicle with lead. Joel was right next to me, and there was a glimmer of hope in his eyes. He rolled onto his back and pointed his gun at the ceiling.

More pops in the near distance. After a few seconds of silence, the blasts opened up with authority. Bullets whizzed through the air. The sound of rounds striking flesh and leaving mortal wounds answered.

After a thirty second barrage, it grew silent again.

"Anyone fucking alive in there?"

"Yeah we're fucking alive!" I yelled back.

"Stay put!" The man's voice was just about the best thing I'd ever heard in my life.

I hoped we were being rescued and not truck-jacked. Even if our would-be heroes wanted all of our shit, maybe they'd leave us alive. A brief moment of horror reminded me of McQuinn's army of jackholes. If they were outside, we were all going to die.

Christy crawled across the floor until she was right next to me. She grasped my hand and held on tightly.

Anna partially covered Roz's body with her own, because Roz kicked her legs up and down, striking the floor in pain. She gurgled something, and then coughed until it sounded like she was going to toss a lung. Anna held Roz's hands to her sides, and didn't let the other woman up.

There were a few more pops of small arms fire, and then someone knocked on the door.

"Don't fucking shoot. We're here to help."

"Yeah okay," I said.

"Don't get too excited, friend."

I smiled. "Sorry, man. We thought we were about to be lunch."

"More like breakfast, but why don't you come out nice and slow and do us a favor--don't show us any guns, if you know what I'm saying. You stay cool and we'll stay cool."

"We're cucumbers," Joel answered.

I looked at him and shook my head. Who says some shit like that?

I rose to my knees and shuffled forward, then stood and peered out, cautiously, at what awaited.

###

06:05 hours approximate
Location: Just outside of Oceanside

The man was probably in his mid-forties, and dressed in battle fatigues. He had dusky skin, and brown eyes that were tight around the corners. He didn't wear any insignia that I could see, but he had a symbol on his collar that looked like a skull with a rifle behind it, and on either side were wings. His face was covered in streaks of dark camouflage. He nodded and I nodded back.

"You folks okay in there?" he asked.

"Mostly," I said.

"We were on patrol and saw the house on fire so we moved in to investigate. Sarge thought a bunch of jumpers on top of a camper meant they were up to nothing good. Not that jumpers need any excuse to be assholes."

I cracked the door open and took in our saviors.

"Thanks for coming along. I thought we were about to join the Zs," I said.

Although I was keeping it cool I was tense, and ready to jump if they made a wrong move.

It was like Kelly and I had a mental connection. I knew without looking that he was lying on the deck and had his AR trained on the door. I knew enough to hit the deck if he yelled "Down!" Not that it would do a lot of good; these guys had enough firepower to wipe us off the face of the earth.

"Name's Ramirez, and we're part of a delta patrol outta Fort Obstacle the third, on account a Fort Obstacle two being overrun a few nights ago," he continued.

I just stared, because a minute ago I'd thought we were all about to join the horde of undead, and now this guy was talking about having multiple fortresses.

"Ramirez, I could just about kiss you," I said.

"You're not my type, but I appreciate the sentiment, sir."

One of the men near him chuckled as he stood around looking like he was about to fall asleep. His weapon was a subcompact; probably an MP5, from the profile. I needed to smack Joel Kelly one of these days, for teaching me to recognize guns on sight.

Five other men who were dressed like our rescuer stood around in a semicircle. One of the guys hanging out to the side had a gun that made Joel's AR look like a toy.

He was on one knee and swinging the barrel around in a short sweep. His eye was pressed to a big scope. He lifted his right hand in the air and raised a digit. The others pointed guns in the direction of his barrel. He lowered his hand, got a finger on the trigger, and then fired. The boom sounded like the sniper rifle that Joel had used when the mercenaries had had us holed up in a hotel a few weeks back.

Behind our men lay several military transports. They idled, with diesel rumbles that were reassuring, to say the least.

"Shit. Jumper swerved, but I think I winged him."

I pressed my hands to the sides of my head as the echo faded into the distance.

"His arm still on?" one of the men in fatigues asked.

"Probably just nicked him. Arm's intact but it ain't gonna work right ever again."

The shooter had a slow Southern drawl. He yanked a soft pack of smokes out of his trouser pocket, shook one out and put it in his mouth before fishing out a lighter.

"That's Perkins. He's pretty good with the long rifle. Thinks he bagged a jumper. Couldn't tell for sure, 'cause the green-eyed asshole fell back into the crowd back there." Ramirez pointed toward the front of the camper.

Joel pushed past me and surveyed the damage.

"What branch are you guys?" he asked.

"Rangers, mostly. It's all mixed company these days. We got a few Marines and some dude from the Air Force who wanted to learn how to shoot."

I chuckled and thought about spilling my story. The difference was I was in the Navy, and didn't want to shoot a goddamn thing for the rest of my life.

"Rangers, eh? What are you guys doing in California?"

"Shooting stuff, mostly," Ramirez said, and wiped his nose. "About two months ago we were sitting around an airport waiting to take off for other parts of the world when the place went batshit. We ended up being a good team, 'cept for Park back there. He hates to change his socks. You can't miss him. He's the big Korean dude."

"Fuck you, I only have two pair," the guy I presumed was Park said.

"Anyway, what are you folks doing out in the middle of the road surrounded by a horde of zulu?"

"Didn't plan it that way," I said. "We were headed for Pendleton when we got stuck in a house. Seems like the shufflers had it in for us."

"Shufflers?"

"Those assholes with green eyes."

"That's pretty good. We call 'em jumpers, because that's what they like to do. Think those fuckers had springs in their feet," Ramirez said.

"We've seen them do some crazy shit," I said.

"So have we. Things are spooky," Ramirez said. "You have a problem, friends. Pendleton fell during the first few days."

Joel stared at the ground for a couple of seconds and didn't say a word.

"Sorry, Joel," I said, but it sounded lame. All of our plans had hinged on reaching Pendleton, reuniting with his Marine brothers, and then going from there. I didn't know what was supposed to happen after that; all I knew was that Joel Kelly had saved my ass and we were in this together.

"Before we start getting too friendly, you guys planning to take our shit?" Joel interrupted. He didn't exactly point his AR-15 at anyone, but he sure seemed like he was going to at any second.

"That wouldn't be very neighborly," Ramirez said. He removed his Kevlar helmet and pushed back his mop of black hair a few times.

"No it would not," Joel said.

I nodded, unsure of what to do. I'd back Joel, of course, because he was generally smarter about these kinds of situations. After McQuinn, I tended to trust nobody.

"We're gathering survivors, and if you all can shoot, that's even more reason to join us. Jumpers are on the move, driving a horde on a couple of outposts, and we need all the help we can get," Ramirez said.

"One of ours is hurt. She was attacked by a shuff--I mean jumper--a half hour ago. Can you do anything for her at this base?" I asked.

Joel stiffened next to me.

"Probably. We have a medical team that stays pretty busy. If we get back before morning mess, we can get her seen. Means we gotta haul ass, though. Are you planning to follow in that piece a shit? No offense to anyone, but it's full a holes and covered in blood and guts," Ramirez said as he looked the vehicle over.

"This is too good to be true." Joel said what I was thinking.

"No sweat if you want to make your own way. We're not exactly in the habit of forcing people to join us. You want to move on, be my guest," Ramirez said. "Probably be in your best interest to take a trip to base. You ask me, we're about the best hope around these parts."

The others checked their weapons or moved around the vehicles, looking over the twice-dead. I couldn't help but feel like they were trying to surround us.

One of the guys took out a huge knife, leaned over, and stabbed a still-moving Z in the head. It took a pair of blows to crack the poor bastard's skull, but after a few seconds it stopped moving.

Anna dropped to the ground next to us and sized up Ramirez.

"Bright Star," she said, pointing at the skull pin on his collar.

"Involuntarily, but yeah," Ramirez nodded. "More like a joint task force. I got recruited a month ago. The rest of us fall under their purview, but for the most part we're peacekeepers." Ramirez shot her a tight smile.

"I'm Lieutenant Commander Sails," she nodded at Ramirez.

He popped a tight salute and then grinned at her. "You could say you're a captain for all I know, but it's good. We get you all back to base and get you sorted and you can start cracking orders. Until then, if you want our help, I'd appreciate it if you did what I asked and when I asked."

"He's okay," Anna said to us. "Unless he took that little symbol off a body. You in the business of looting and killing?"

"No ma'am. We're a little rough around the edges but we're good guys. 'Cept Park. He's real grumpy because he hasn't had kimchee in a few weeks. Personally I think the stuff is disgusting. Give me some crap bastardized Mexican food any day. Know what I miss most? You're gonna laugh. I miss Taco Time. Worst excuse for Mexican food in the entire world but it used to taste like fucking heaven."

I practically started to drool.

"Just like that?" Joel asked. "He comes in, says a few nice things, and we're going to trust these guys."

"Hey man, we just saved you," the guy with the big knife said. "A little gratitude would be appreciated."

"Not saying we're not grateful, just cautious. We've had problems," Joel said. "The worst shit in the world brings out the worst shit in people."

"We all got problems, brother. There's a bunch of quasi-dead fucks out there with a taste for meat and we're their main food source. We'll just leave you to your business. Have a good night, folks."

"Cook, that was some action hero line there, taste for meat, someone give this guy an Oscar,"

Ramirez chuckled.

"I'm just here to chew bubble gum and kick some ass. I'm all out of bubble gum," Cook said.

"Fucking shoot me now," Ramirez sighed.

06:25 hours approximate
Location: Just outside of Oceanside

Ramirez nodded at one of his companions and together they moved into formation.

"Wait," Anna said. "Tell us where we're going and we'll follow."

"Make up your frigging minds. We're about ten miles from base and it's a *long* ten with all those zulu and crap littering the roads. You want to follow us and we'll lead you to Obstacle Charlie. You check in and go about your business and we'll go about ours. But we don't know you all from Adam, so I'd appreciate it if you follow my lead. Sound good?"

I didn't know what to say. These guys had saved us, but we didn't know the first thing about them except that they seemed to operate out of some mythical base that was all puppy dogs and unicorn rainbows.

"Let's get the truck running and go with them," Joel said. "If Pendleton is toast then we don't have anywhere else to go, except to find a new home and wait for it to get overrun. Besides, these guys have enough firepower to take us out in a couple of seconds. If they wanted to kill us they would have done it already."

"Good point, I guess," I grumbled.

"Let's just get this rig moving and see where the day takes us," Anna said.

Roz thrashed once, then curled up in a ball. I moved to the door to check on her. She had her hands clenched to her stomach like they were holding in her guts. Her head whipped back so hard I thought she was going to snap her neck.

Ramirez poked his head inside the camper, then pushed past us. Anna reacted with a "Wait!" but he was already up the stairs. He slipped on a couple of spent shells, shoved aside a bag of canned goods, and dropped beside Roz.

Anna shoved herself into the space next to him and kept her hand on her sidearm. I moved into the camper as well, my wrench in hand.

"Tell me what happened to her again?" He pushed aside her hair and studied the wounds on her face.

"She got jumped by one of the green-eyes. I didn't see it bite her, but he was busy trying to rip her mouth open or something. The blood might not all be hers, and the wounds don't seem that bad."

He set a hand next to her, avoiding the glob of puke she'd spit up, and leaned in to peel back an eyelid. He slipped off a glove and felt her head.

"Did he put something in her mouth?"

"Dude. Why the fuck would a shuffler put

something in her mouth?" I said.

He moved his hand down and pressed on her chest as she thrashed against his grip. She snarled and then her head snapped back again, hitting the floor hard enough to shake the camper.

"Don't know, but our mission just got more interesting. We need to get her back to the base as soon as possible."

"Damn straight," I said.

Ramirez triggered a mic near his neck and spoke a few commands. Men moved in and helped Roz and me down from the door. They weren't disrespectful, and when they got inside the camper they were very gentle with our friend.

A medic pushed aside one of the men and inspected the wounds on Roz's face. He ripped a Velcro closure and extracted a white package from a belt pouch. The medic took a pile of gauze and pressed it over Roz's wounds.

We were pushed out of the camper, and ended up huddling together. The clouds had been fat and grey, and I guess they'd decided they'd had enough of this day, because rain pissed down on us--sprinkles at first, before water fell in earnest.

"She's going to be okay, Joel," I said, and put a hand on his shoulder. I tried to forget his harsh words in the vehicle, but they still stung.

He shrugged me off, and moved to consult with one of the men who carried a submachine gun.

"Alright. We got our extract path cleared, now

if this rig don't start, how do you feel about leaving it behind?"

Like most anything I'd gotten halfway attached to in this new world, I wasn't all that keen on leaving our home behind. It wasn't even that I *liked* the piece of shit. It was just familiar, in what was about to become all-new and unfamiliar.

A mini-horde of Zs broke from cover and shambled toward us. The men around Ramirez were quick and dropped them one by one with timed shots. No one panicked; they just took care of business.

I shook my head to calm the ringing in my ears.

"We gotta call it, and soon. Many more Zs and we're just attracting attention with all of the shooting," one of Ramirez's men said.

"We have a lot of supplies in the truck," I said.

I moved to the front of the vehicle and inspected the damage. Blood, bits of clothing, and body parts were jammed into the grill. Most of the front end was crushed, and the bumper held on for dear life by a couple of bolts.

Frosty sat in the driver's seat like she was out for a Sunday drive. Her ears perked up when the new guys appeared next to me, and her lips rose. She issued a half-hearted growl.

I helped a guy pluck chunks out of the front of the truck. We both grimaced but took care of business. Another guy popped the hood and we looked at the engine. There was enough blood, guts, and chunks of stuff that resembled flesh to make a couple of horror movies.

"Cute dog," he said.

"Yeah she's cool. Likes to taunt Zs. Dog's been great on guard duty," I said.

I wasn't about to give them an excuse to leave her behind.

"Shit. I think that's half a hand stuck in the belt," I said, and grabbed a piece of clothing that had to have been a sleeve.

The sleeve *was* attached to a hand. The hand was jammed between a belt and a gear. Extracting the mess was an exercise I hoped to never repeat.

"Fire it up," my companion called.

The engine cranked, tried to turn over and died.

"We gotta call it," Ramirez yelled.

I looked around the side of the truck. His men were falling back into military transports that had appeared. They were drab shades of tan; they would have fit right in if we'd been engaged in Afghanistan.

More chunks, so I yanked them out as fast as I could. Bits of flesh were jammed in the radiator but there wasn't a whole lot I could do, short of hosing it down with a pressure washer.

They tried to start the engine again but it choked again.

"Fuck," I said in frustration.

"Hey man, we tried. Let's get the hell out of here before the main horde arrives," Cooper said.

"Main horde?"

"Yeah, be here in about an hour. We were scouting them when we came across the burning house. Good thing we came along. This bunch weren't nothing compared to the shitstorm's about to arrive."

I kicked the front of the truck a few times, hoping to loosen more crap. The man in the truck kept cranking, but it was no use.

"We're out of time. Delta squad, mount up," Ramirez called.

"Let's go, man." Cooper grabbed my sleeve and pulled.

A fresh batch of newly-undead broke from cover and came at us. I picked up my wrench, ready to bash heads to relieve some tension.

"That's just great," I muttered.

The men moved around me and then jogged toward the transports. I stared after them with contempt, because I was sure the truck would start if we took a few more minutes.

I kicked the grill again and then hit it with my wrench. The only thing that happened was the bumper gave up and hit the ground. I picked it up and lifted it over my head. "Screw you, Zs," I said, and flung it. The part fell well short and clattered across the pavement.

I stalked toward our new companions and wondered what we were in for.

#

Reavers

06:55 hours approximate
Location: Just outside of Oceanside

The first order of business was to get Frosty out of the truck. She growled at the military guys, but they were flesh and living blood, so after a little coaxing she began to enjoy the attention. Most of the guys cautiously approached her and took turns patting her head. A few found treats in their pockets and bribed friendship.

Our new friends put Roz in the back of a military truck. When Joel tried to join her they politely, but firmly, pointed him in the direction of a HMMWV-looking beast of a truck. We piled in and I was reminded of our escape from the military hospital a month or so ago. We'd fled, Joel and I holding on for dear life while a gunner shot the Zs that pursued us.

When there was a break in the action, the warriors took turns inspecting weapons, reloading, and playing grab-ass. A woman with a scar across her face smacked a guy's hand away and then punched him in the chest, but she smiled and said something that made him laugh.

Joel and I took turns showing off our dog tags to Ramirez so we looked legit. One of the guys shook his head and looked away with a snort. Joel dug out a battered wallet and extracted his military ID. I had mine around here somewhere, but it was probably buried in the bottom of my bag. Ramirez looked Joel's over, looked at him a few times and then shook his hand.

"What's wrong with that guy who looked like someone pissed in his Cheerios?" I asked Joel after he and Ramirez were done with their little bonding moment.

"Could be we took the tags off a couple of dead bodies. He doesn't know us and we look like shit. When's the last time we tried to look like we belong in the military? That's why I dug out my ID."

"Who's got time for that Mickey Mouse bullshit? I'm glad to wake up every day. Shaving would be nice, sure, so would a shower, and a turkey and mashed potato dinner. None of that shit's gonna happen anytime soon."

Anna approached Ramirez and took him to the side. They spoke together for several minutes while she dug out a beat-up looking wallet and showed him the contents. Whatever she put in front of his face must have triggered something, because he nodded at her and then they both got very serious.

I drifted toward them, hoping to catch a hint of what the mysterious Anna Sails said, but she shot me a look and I gave up on learning her secrets.

Joel stowed his assault rifle in the back of a rig under the watchful eye of one of the men. I kept my wrench at my side and my gun in its holster. If they decided they needed to take our weapons, I was sure Anna and Joel would have a few choice words for them. Besides, we were outnumbered by a healthy margin, and we had a kid with us. As far as threats went, we were slightly above sad puppies.

Joel shook hands with a couple of men and crawled in the back of their vehicle. I tried to wave at him, to offer a half-assed flag of apology for our words earlier, but I didn't think he saw me.

Frosty stuck to Christy and followed her to our vehicle, licking every hand in sight as she passed soldiers. The woman with the scar on her face dropped to a crouch and cautiously pulled our dog into an embrace. Frosty looked at me with her big eyes, tongue lolling out as she waited patiently for the woman to let go.

Anna was done with her pep talk and joined us. She didn't meet my eye, but got into the back of the transport and settled in. She looked cool as she stared out the window. She had a look on her face I hadn't seen very often over the last few weeks: she was determined.

"I don't suppose you want to share your conversation with Ramirez?" I leaned over and whispered.

"I don't suppose you want to mind your own fucking business?" she shot back.

I bit off a retort when Christy crawled over Anna and sat between us. Frosty followed her and took up most of the floor space under Anna. Anna didn't mind, and told Frosty she was a good girl.

Christy looked very small and afraid. I dropped an arm around her shoulder and pulled her into me. She hugged me back.

"Are we going to be safe now?" Christy asked me.

"I hope so. I'm sick and tired of being on the run all the time."

"What if these guys aren't good and they want to, you know, *do* stuff to us?" Christy whispered.

"Then they'll have to go through me," I whispered back, trying to sound tough.

The rest of the crew piled into vehicles. Then someone gave a signal and we lurched into motion.

"What's the base like?" I asked our driver.

"Like a brick fucking fortress, brother. We got the Seabees to build the walls and they're about ten feet high. Got heavy equipment blocking some of the entrances. Talk about zulu-stoppers, this thing is meant to *sustain*. Regular choppers come in and drop supplies during the week. Then we got water coming in on the weekends. Sometimes we got us a surplus and you can even take a shower."

I didn't catch the guy's name, but he was sitting next to Ramirez. Ramirez, for his part, had stopped being Chatty Cathy. If he had anything to interject about us or where we were going, he kept his mouth shut.

"How long has Obstacle, what was it, Echo, been there?"

"Outpost Obstacle Charlie. Been there for over a month now and we've repelled the best the goddamn jumpers threw at us, plus the Reavers. The worst assault was a week or so ago. We held our own and left a pile of bodies. Worst part was cleanup," he said.

"That's not the first time I've heard about the Reavers. Who are they?"

"Crazies, man. They want to run a cult or something--least, that's what I hear from up high. They fight the Zs, but they have a hard-on for those green-eyed bastards. I also heard they're working with the jumpers."

I shook my head. "So how'd the other bases go down?" I asked.

The man looked at Ramirez. The two exchanged a look, but the southerner didn't answer, and neither did Ramirez.

"Name's Cook, by the way. Freddy Cook."

We made our introductions. Sails did her thing where her voice changed as she announced she was a lieutenant commander.

"Well, ma'am. Sure is nice to have you all along for the ride," he said, and then went silent again.

We poked along roads, avoiding wrecks. Ramirez kept speaking into his microphone and advising which routes to avoid. We came across a mound of bodies, and everyone looked away. We passed a freeway entrance that was blocked by a semi that had crashed into the rail. Another car was wedged under the wreck.

The truck bumped over debris, and slowed when there was a pile-up ahead.

We moved away from the rural area and skirted a couple of shopping centers. Zs littered the roads and sidewalks--some moving, but most lying in heaps on the ground. There were a couple of times when I thought I saw green eyes regarding us, but I couldn't be sure in the light of day.

The driver found a back road and took to it at speed. We rolled past apartment buildings and gas stations, coffee stands, and convenience stores, all of which lay like wrecks of society. The few Zs we spotted kept to themselves.

We'd gone a few more miles when something in the distance caught my eye.

"What the hell is that?" Anna said, pointing out the disturbance.

Our ride slowed, because the vehicle ahead of us decelerated. Joel kept his eyes on the truck behind us, because Roz was in it. Ramirez said something into his microphone, and we all pulled over.

In the distance, something burned. We'd just left a fucking pile of ash behind us, and now there was a fire ahead.

Ramirez issued orders over his microphone. A couple of guys got out of the head vehicle and went to investigate.

"What's happening up there?" I asked.

"Might be civvies got stuck. Going to take a look," Ramirez said.

"What if it's Reavers?" I asked.

Anna snorted.

"What?" I argued. "Sounds like a bunch of wackos out there. Remember McQuinn?"

"I remember him well enough. I also remember that he got his ass kicked," Anna said.

"Bad stuff happens when the world goes to hell, man. People forget what it's like to be civilized. Luckily, part of the military survived and got organized. That's why we set up these bases and the battle lines. First month, it was all about survival. Now it's all about reestablishing order," Ramirez said.

Soldiers got out of trucks and set up a perimeter while a couple of them scouted ahead.

"What happened right after the outbreak? We've been on the run for a long time and we were on a ship when it all went down," I said.

"Not much to tell. World went to shit. Zulus became the enemy, as well as everyone's neighbor. When the power went out, that was the worst. You'd hear screaming and gunfire all night. Rapes, murders, it was like medi-fucking-eval times, brother. There were a lot more of us, but a lot of uniforms left and went looking for families. Some of us stayed and waited for order to be restored."

"Glad you all stuck it out. We've been playing hide and seek for weeks, and it sucked," I said.

"Yeah, man. I feel ya. Once we started establishing bases, there was an initiative put forward to clear the cities. Not easy, trust me on that one. We set up patrols that went out and made a lot of noise. They'd fall back, with a horde of the enemy in pursuit. Once they reached the line, we went to work and put them down. Set up big ditches and did the dirty deed. Thing was, we didn't have to shoot them all. Big old bulldozers moved in and pushed the bodies into the pits."

I shuddered.

"What happened to the Zs after that?" Joel said.

"We buried 'em under rocks and ten feet of dirt. Sometimes we demolished buildings and put the rubble in the tombs. Don't know how many we've put in the ground, but it's a lot."

Visions of Nazis stuffing graves with Jewish bodies filled my mind.

"That is fucked up," I said.

"The worst thing is that it's not even one percent of the dead. We have a long way to go."

It wasn't what I meant, but I let it go. No sense in arguing with our would-be rescuers.

The large truck that had been following

maneuvered around us and then sped up the street.

I leaned forward and said, "Wait, Roz is in that truck."

"It's okay. Road's been cleared all the way back to base, and they need to get her into medical right away. We'll just take a look and then follow them," Ramirez answered.

"Will she be okay?" I asked.

He looked at me but didn't say a word.

"Any of you guys got .357 ammo?" Anna asked.

"I think Park has some, but he's in the other truck. We got a bunch of 5.56 and some .40. Thing is--and I'm not going to beat around the bush here, friends--we'd prefer if ya'll keep your weapons holstered. Now, I'm not saying you're bad people, but this is a bad world, and a bad world makes people do bad things."

He was right about that.

"We're not going to do anything stupid," Anna said.

"Didn't say you were, just stating that we all want to stay friends."

I sat back in my seat and stared out the window at the departing truck.

Ramirez got out, but Cook stayed in the running automobile. Anna was close behind Ramirez as he hit the ground. I sat for a few seconds, then decided that I didn't like the idea of sitting on my ass, so I followed them.

"Jackson?" Christy asked.

"Hang loose, dude. I'll be right back."

"What should I do?"

"Don't shoot anyone unless you have to, and keep an eye on that mongrel dog of ours," I added with a wink. Thing was, I wasn't leaving Christy alone in the vehicle with someone I didn't know. I stood near the door and kept an eye on Christy, but I also unlimbered my wrench.

Another transport came to a halt, and men popped out until there were five surrounding us. They moved crisply, and their gear and clothes, for the most part, were clean. Something I hadn't seen in a long time was military precision. These guys actually gave me hope.

07:10 hours approximate
Location: Just outside of Oceanside

Ramirez gathered his men up into a semi-circle and said a few words to them. He issued orders, checked on the status of his team, and asked questions about the fire. I found a free section of truck and leaned against it.

The respite was welcomed; we'd been running on pure adrenaline for the last few hours, and now my energy was fading. I wanted to sleep, so I took a deep breath, leaned back and closed my eyes for a few seconds.

Voices whispered around me as I drifted. Faces

flashed, and memories of our flight from the house flooded my sleep-deprived mind.

Someone screamed in the distance, but I shook my head and fled from the horrors we'd seen over the last few days.

I closed my eyes again, but not for long.

Gunfire rattled me out half-sleep into full fucking alert. My heart hammered in my chest as more guns opened fire around us. Something clattered off the door, and that made me hit the deck.

Joel stood by the second transport, but when shots echoed, he moved into action. He reached into the back of the vehicle and tugged his assault rifle out of storage. Joel moved quickly toward the front of the car. The driver had already popped out of his seat and was looking for targets, gun at high ready.

A couple of guys took up station along the side of the road and pointed their guns. I stood around with my dick in my hands, wondering what to do. Gunfire? Check. Unknown assailants? Check.

I stayed next to the vehicle and tried to be small.

Rounds clattered across the back of the second vehicle. Joel lifted his rifle and aimed, but I couldn't tell what he was looking for. I risked a glance over the door, but all I saw were shadowy figures in the distance, moving away from the fire. They were armed, but I wasn't sure if they were friend or foe.

Ramirez yelled into his headset, looking for his team. He called to them several times.

"What's the word?" Joel yelled.

I decided that my word was "Get the fuck into the fight," and took out the XDM. Anna skirted the front of the vehicle until she reached my position.

Frosty growled from within the truck.

Men deployed from one of the other vehicles, dropping to the side of the road. They moved next to a low line of grass and took aim at the figures moving toward us.

A bullet whizzed overhead. I spun and tried to find the source, but I felt very much like a bug under a flyswatter I couldn't see coming.

Ramirez dropped to his knee, lifted his assault rifle, and fired in the direction of the houses along our side. Someone returned fire, so I hit the deck. Anna was right next to me. She pulled her Smith & Wesson and aimed.

"Who the hell is shooting at us?" I asked.

She shook her head.

"Suppressing fire there," Ramirez yelled and pointed at a house. "I want a line of fire on our six. Collins, and Mertz, don't shoot until you're sure, but when you're sure, make it count. I'm ready to call it but we need to hear back from our patrol."

"Got it, Sarge," one of the guys called back.

"Perkins, find me some targets and erase them. Park, set up the big gun."

I thought about hiding under the vehicle, but with my luck I'd probably get run over as soon as they decided to haul ass.

"I got movement at ten o'clock. I'm going to drop them unless it's our patrol," Joel said.

"We don't know yet," Ramirez said.

I hustled to the rear of the vehicle and put Joel between me and them. I'd taken out my 9mm, but no one had told me which direction to shoot in.

I held the 9mm next to my chest, hoping a target would present itself. Ramirez squatted next to me and screamed orders into his headset. It was all "Move here, bring in guys there, cover this, and cover that." He called for support and got a positive response, based on his tone. This was all very reassuring, because I didn't think I could clench my butt cheeks any tighter if I tried.

"Suppressive fire!" yelled Park and turned his gun on a house at our ten o'clock.

Joel Kelly joined in and ripped a few shots at windows. Glass shattered and holes appeared. I'd never in my entire life wanted to be hidden inside a tank until this moment.

One of the guys in the lead vehicle hit the ground and ran to an outcropping of rock. He slid behind cover and quickly popped up and fired. Another man was hot on his heels and slid next to him.

"Movement at three o'clock," someone yelled.

"Let 'em pass. That's Eakins and Ellis back from scouting the fire. When they get here we are going to evac. Cooper, lay down some smoke."

"You got it, boss," Cooper said.

"More movement on our twelve," one of the men called.

Ramirez did a quick scan of the area.

"Alright, gents, we have no more than ten hostiles. I want them put down. Ellis and Eakins, flank that low hill. You see anyone in black, you put 'em down. Park, I want you taking down targets in those houses. Cook, you and me are going to lead the assault."

"Assault?" I swallowed.

"Just stay here and try not to get shot," Ramirez said.

Joel tagged along with Ramirez and Cook as they moved out. The three moved quickly, assault rifles on shoulders as they ran.

A Reaver got brave, popped up and fired on the men, but he shot wildly. He didn't get a chance to fire another volley; he was blown off his feet when Joel Kelly put a pair of bullets through his chest.

A couple of figures fled the house and ran across the street. Park opened fire on their location and tagged one. He fell to the ground, his buddy dropping next to him, then fired a few rounds in our direction.

Park hit the ground, and before he could return fire, the pair had hobbled around the side of another house. Park didn't give up, and shot at the location for a few seconds. The men did not reappear.

The helicopter thumped overhead as it took up

station. The Reavers must have decided they'd had enough, because they turned and ran. More gunfire was exchanged.

Cooper pulled a pair of grenades from his pack and handed one to Joel. They nodded at each other and almost in unison pulled pins and tossed. A pair of pops echoed and then smoke rolled out and began to cover us from the houses.

"Second floor window, more movement," one of the men behind the rock called.

His partner, Park, turned his big-ass machine gun on the area and opened up. Whatever he was using to shoot with required the gun to have a bipod deployed from near the barrel of the gun. He grabbed it, and it looked like he was holding on for dear life as it rattled. His partner dropped to the side with his hands pressed to his ears as guns boomed.

The window and surrounding wall became shattered glass and shards of wood as rounds punched into the home. Someone screamed, but not for very long.

The gunner shifted his aim and lit up another section of the house.

"Fall back, Ellis and Eakins are here. We're moving out," Ramirez yelled.

His men moved fast, grabbing gear, slinging guns, keeping low, and moving to the vehicles. All told, it couldn't have taken more than ten seconds for them to get back into the trucks and prepare to drive us anywhere but here.

Anna stormed around the side of our truck, then paused to stare hard at something in the low outcropping of shrub near us. She lifted her revolver, and a pair of rounds snapped smartly.

"More shufflers, but they are so damn fast," she said as she got back in the truck.

"Shufflers?" I huffed as I got back in the truck and slid next to Christy.

Frosty kept her head down, ears down, and tail tucked. I didn't blame her one bit.

As we piled in, she shrunk into the seat and huddled next to me. The lead vehicle moved out with ours close behind before doors had been shut.

A helicopter buzzed overhead, passed us, and then came back. I half-expected that it would fire on us, but instead it swung to the side and a rattling filled the air. We were a good twenty-five feet away, and expended rounds clattered across the pavement as a machine gun opened up. The front of a house blew inward. The shooter paused and shot again, blowing part of the second house to smithereens.

We were already on the move, but figures in black garb popped up on one side of the road. They were armed with machine guns and rocket launchers. I thought it was amazing that a full task force had arrived to help us--until they started shooting.

###

Battle Lines

07:45 hours approximate
Location: Just outside of Oceanside

The men reminded me of the crew that had been guarding the old woman's shop back in town--garbed from head to toe in black. Their ski masks didn't do much except add to the fact that they looked like assholes.

One thing I noticed was that they were somewhat uncoordinated. Not that *I* was an expert of military strategy, but these guys sort of ran to the edge of a hill and dropped. One of the men was a little overweight and tripped, nearly dropping his gun.

I stifled a laugh when several assault rifles turned on us.

"Who the fuck…" I didn't get to finish my sentence before they fired on us.

"Down," Ramirez screamed.

The truck ahead of us swerved and was hit by machine gun fire. An RPG round roared, but missed them and sailed away on a tail of smoke. It impacted with an apartment building and exploded, raining debris on the ground. Chunks rattled across the roof of our ride.

No offense to whoever built our vehicle, but a round that size would send us to a fiery death.

The helicopter turned and swept toward our position.

Rounds punched into the side of our truck. Christy screamed, so I grabbed her and pushed her into Anna, making them sink lower into the seat. Frosty moaned, but there was nothing I could do for the dog except keep her from freaking the fuck out.

The driver turned his head to take in the threat. Glass shattered as a round shattered a window. The driver jerked and slumped to the side. Ramirez leaned over and grabbed the wheel to steady the truck.

"Cook, Cook, hit it, man," Ramirez said.

I thought the driver was dead, but he jammed his foot into the floor and the truck responded by leaping forward.

The helicopter opened up with a pair of rocket rounds that exploded into the ground around the guys assaulting us.

I ran my hand over my arm and side to make sure I wasn't hit, because the shockwave felt like it took a layer of skin off.

"Shoot back," Anna said and handed me her gun. She put an arm protectively around Christy and held her close.

I took the gun and sat up. Figures swarmed before me. I aimed and pulled the trigger, and regretted the blast that echoed around the interior. I clearly missed, so I guessed at the way the truck was darting and led my next target with the reticules. The gun boomed in my hands and a man slumped to the side, catching his friend and dragging him to the ground. I fired again and missed.

"I suck at this," I muttered.

"You did great, Creed," Anna said.

We'd moved past the line of shooters, most of whom were scattering now that we had air support. Another truck took a turn and came up behind us. I thought it was one of our guys, but when bullets peppered the back of the car, I realized they were also gunning for us.

Ramirez screamed more orders into his headset. I wished I could shoot back, but the rear of the vehicle was closed off and angled downward. The engineer part of my brain told me that it was probably designed to deflect shots, and the want-to-stay-alive part of my brain warned me that with enough power, a bunch of rounds would turn us into spaghetti.

The helicopter swung around again and opened fire on the pursuing truck. Thank the fuck Christ for the boys in that bird. If not for them, we'd have been toast.

Ramirez yanked the wheel hard to avoid an abandoned car. We swiped the truck's side, but managed to stay on the road.

Bullets hit the truck again, and we nearly went off the road when the driver overcorrected. Anna came out of the seat, still holding Christy. She slapped her hand against the roof and pushed them both back down.

I'd nearly dropped the gun as I reached for them both. Anna shot me a look of consternation, so I handed her pistol back. She took it, and then swiveled to her side and pressed her left arm against the door. She popped up out of the remains of the window, brushing aside safety glass on her way.

The helicopter skewed away from us and then spun hard. I caught the shadow as the blades cut into the sunlight, fuselage temporarily hiding the sun. The truck pursuing us took a small road that was covered with trees.

Something rocketed across the sky, trailing smoke. The chopper swerved, hard to port, and the missile flew by.

"What the fuck is going on out there?" I yelled.

The figure of Joel Kelly appeared in the truck ahead of us. He came out of the window and braced his upper body against the window. Anna on our left side, Joel on the lead vehicle's right, me holding onto a little girl. That pretty much summed up my life.

Joel must have taken issue with something ahead. He aimed, and fired rapidly. I knew that guy pretty well. He was usually calm, and reserved ammo whenever possible, so he must have been pissed.

Something slammed into the truck--*several* somethings. The driver held onto his side and groaned, but he and Ramirez kept the truck from running off the road.

The chopper faded back as another something whistled through the air. I hesitated to even call them missiles, because we were the *good* guys, right? We were the men and women fighting the hordes of Zs. This new world might suck, but it didn't have the right to throw *this* at us.

Ramirez cocked his head to the side. "Our air support is pulling back until they figure out who the hell is firing on them," he said over his shoulder.

"Then who's going to cover us?" I asked.

"You figure that out, I'll give you a gold fucking star."

"Great. Always wanted to be an admiral," I said, trying to sound like a smartass. Truth was, I was scared to death. We were in a high-speed tin can, being fired on by unknown assailants.

"No worries, we're close to the base now. Should be just over that rise," Ramirez said.

Joel emptied another magazine and then popped back into the truck.

Something took shape in the road. More guys in uniform? I strained to make out who they were, and realized there were a bunch of Zs with a couple of shufflers guiding them. The only good news was that they were facing away from us. So who were they after?

08:20 hours approximate
Location: Just outside of Oceanside

The day was gray and the sky was fat with clouds. Looked like it was about to piss rain on this part of the state. The landscape around us was a mess of dilapidated buildings that had probably been high-end stores a few months ago. Now they were battered and abused. Doors hung open, windows had been shattered, and mannequins, boxes, clothes, bags, and all kinds of crap were scattered among a host of roving Zs.

We'd pulled ahead of the battle and, I hoped, away from the guys shooting at us for good. After the battle at the house, I'd had enough of guys firing on me to get through the next six months.

A pair of pickups cut across the road and roared off to a side street. Joel aimed and fired. It wasn't until later that I thought to even ask if he knew who he was shooting at.

A third vehicle followed. It was a big Chevy Tahoe that had been spray-painted with green and gray. The windows were darkened, but the rear one cracked open, slid down, and revealed a guy with a machine gun. He leaned out and fired on the lead vehicle. Joel fired back and then popped back into the truck.

"Shoot back, Creed," Anna said.

The SUV roared away and followed the other trucks.

"They're gone," I said lamely.

The helicopter reappeared and squatted over our position. Ramirez shouted commands into his mic.

Our truck slowed to a crawl and the chopper kept pace over us. Then it must have gotten the green light to pursue, because it flew after the trucks.

"Why are they fucking around and shooting at us?" I asked.

"Million dollar question. Best we can figure, given reports at base, they're launching a full-scale assault on Fort Obstacle. We're to get back with a quickness and bring some thunder."

"Hooah," Cook said.

A pair of cars roared up on us, *Mad Max*-style. They were modified SUVs fitted with some kind of armor plating. They came parallel with us, and gunfire sounded. We got low in the backseat as rounds exploded around Joel's truck.

The HMMWV swerved onto the road and we followed, Cook fighting the wheel as he spun so hard I nearly turned Christy into a pancake.

More gunfire rattled around us, and that's when our salvation came into sight.

The base was just as they'd described it: walls had been set up in a semi-circle around a couple of buildings. Along the perimeter sat four taller lookout stations that couldn't have been more than thirty feet high. The walls were lined with razor wire and spikes. Along the wall lay piles of the dead.

A bulldozer sat near a curb, hulking and cold. Yellow paint had peeled in places, and the scoop was a dark red. I didn't need anyone to explain to me that it was dyed that color from blood.

Something in the distance caught my attention. I struggled to make out what I was seeing. Like a black wave, it shuddered as it strode the ground. "Massive" didn't even begin to describe it. I rubbed my eyes, shook my head, and squinted. Optical illusion brought on by smoke and adrenaline? An army of bad guys on the move?

I knew what it was, but my mind sank into the land of denial.

Something whistled five feet off the deck and exploded as it struck one of the walls. The East side was under assault, and entire sections had been blown away. A piece of heavy machinery moved into place and pushed the remains of the wall back into place. Then, it stopped. A couple of guys in green hopped out, firing into the distance as they hit the ground.

"Fucking Reavers," breathed Ramirez.

The helicopter flashed across the sky, having hopefully dealt with the trucks, and came to hover just over the base. It swept left and then paused so the gunner could concentrate fire on a location to the East.

Assault rifles hammered in the morning air.

"What the hell is going on?" was all I could manage. *Brilliant.*

"I'm scared, Jackson," Christy said.

I pulled her close and told her I was also scared, but that didn't help. She probably wanted me to go all Joel Kelly and figure out how to shoot the bad guys.

That's when the morning was shaken by an explosion that smashed into Joel's truck. The vehicle tilted a full three feet and then slammed to the ground. The force of the explosion pushed the truck off the road and into the gutter.

"IED!" Cook yelled.

They brought the truck to a fast halt, and Ramirez and Cook poured out. The truck behind us slammed on its brakes, and more men filled the street. They set up a perimeter while our driver and Ramirez ran to the truck.

Joel fell out, looking dazed and confused. He held his hand to his ear, but damn if that tough Marine still kept his AR in one hand. He sat down hard in the middle of the street and looked around. His eyes were unfocused and he shook his head. Blood dripped from his hands.

I was already out of the truck and on my way to help Joel. Something whistled over the ground and then roared past me. The RPG round smashed into the truck behind us and exploded. I hit the ground hard enough to see stars and the breath left my body. I rolled over, ears ringing, and stared at the sky.

Christy and Anna fell out of our truck, followed by Frosty, and made for me.

"Ambush, get off the street," Ramirez yelled.

A man near me dropped, and didn't move again. More gunfire rattled around me.

Anna was the last out. She helped me up, and together we stumbled to the side of the road, with Christy and Frosty hot on our heels. Anna held her pistol as we bolted for cover.

I felt dazed, like someone had punched me upside the head. My ears still rang and I got a case of vertigo so strong I dropped to my hands and knees.

"Get up, Creed. Get the fuck up and head for the trees," Anna yelled, but her voice sounded hollow, like she was yelling inside a room filled with mattresses.

Christy grabbed my arm and pulled. I looked up, and her face was frozen in shock. She yelled at me, but I couldn't understand her. Frosty nipped at Christy's arm, but she pushed the dog away.

I rolled over and struggled to breathe. Bullets

rattled around me, so I hit the deck again. Always make yourself a small target: that was Joel's advice.

Ramirez turned and returned fire. He laid a line of fire on a building across from us. Rounds punched into walls and shattered windows. The roar of gunfire was a muddled mess in my head.

I got to my hands and knees again and decided that I didn't want to be a target, so I staggered--yeah, just like a Z--toward an apartment building that looked as if fire had taken it a few weeks ago. Christy stuck to me, and Frosty ran ahead.

We reached a caved-in doorway and dropped next to a set of concrete stairs. I reached for my gun, but it wasn't there. My backpack was in the rear of the truck, and with it, my backup weapon. The only things I had on me were a knife and my trusty wrench. I knew the heavy tool was still strapped under my arm, because I'd felt every bang as it repeatedly struck my ribs and side.

Christy pushed Frosty down and together we huddled while the air filled with bullets.

08:20 hours approximate
Location: Just outside of Oceanside

A round kicked up dirt near me, so I grabbed Christy's hand and we dodged into the darkness the doorway offered. We stuck to walls, and stepped over debris and the remains of the door.

I poked my head around the corner and found that the military had set up a line of fire and were giving back as much as they'd taken. It was like a scene from a documentary on the battles in Afghanistan. They ducked and moved, found cover, and fired back.

The wave continued to advance. They weren't headed directly for us; more at an angle that might keep them off our path. The thing in *their* direct path, however, was Fort Obstacle.

I caught Joel's shape and noticed that he'd given up his AR in favor of the big rifle Park had carried, which didn't bode well for him. Joel dug in next to a tree, lifted the big weapon and fired. The boom echoed around the battlefield.

Perkins appeared next to Joel and yelled something in his ear. Joel nodded and fell back.

The thumping of a helicopter sounded, and a big one appeared. It was fat and had a flat bottom. A guy manned a machine gun and unleashed a few hundred rounds. A building fifty yards away took the brunt of the gunfire. Walls blew inward, and glass and wood fell.

The chopper hovered low, then nearly touched the ground.

Ramirez strode to the truck we'd arrived in. He yelled commands and waved hand gestures at his remaining men.

Something moaned in the darkness behind us.

"Creed, I think there's a Z in here," Christy said.

I made the mistake of lingering near the doorway, and a couple of bullets struck the wood above me. I grabbed Christy and we moved into the building. It was either face a Z or try to run back to the truck while we were shot at.

Anna and Joel wouldn't leave us behind. They were probably on the way now.

The first apartment door had been caved in. The room was filled with overturned furniture and a pair of rotting bodies.

"We need to find a way out the back. Keep Frosty close," I whispered.

Christy nodded.

A pair of doors on either side of us had also been broken in. We found more of the same: overturned rooms, clothes in heaps, dishes smashed on the floor, and blood.

The helicopter fired a few more times, and then the thump of blades faded as the chopper departed the area.

08:30 hours approximate
Location: Just outside of Oceanside

The Z stumbled out of a doorway and right smack into me.

I managed to push him back, but he was a *hungry* fucker. His milky white eyes fixed on me. He wore a bathrobe that had probably been tan at one time. Now it was the same color as the shitty apartment he'd been hanging out in: blood and dirt.

He grabbed my arm and I swung him around and into the wall. He struck it, and then stumbled right back into me. Following the explosion I was still rattled; it was all I could do to keep him from getting his head in close.

Frosty was having none of this. The dog grabbed his robe, growled low in her throat, and thrashed her head from side to side as she pulled him off me.

Christy picked up a chunk of wood and pushed him back into the room.

He tripped over the remains of his door and fell over. Legs kicked, and feet scrambled for purchase. Frosty bit at his ankle and shook him again. I pulled her off, and then motioned for Christy to step back.

I unlimbered my wrench, and when the Z turned and started to crawl toward me, I swung hard and smashed his head to a pulp, but it took every ounce of energy. The entire morning was crashing in on me. Fleeing from the house, surrounded on all sides by Zs, shooting from moving vehicles, and the attack on our rescuers. It was too much. I wanted to find a little room, curl up in a ball, and sleep for about three days.

"We need to get out of here now," I told Christy.

"I know. I'm scared, Jackson. Can we please find Anna and Joel?"

"That's the order of business, but someone's shooting at us from the front of the building. We need to find a way out the back," I said, and grabbed her hand and tugged her behind me.

She nodded as we moved, and offered me her revolver. I looked at the little weapon.

"Hang onto it, dude. If things get hairy you know how to use it. I'll stick to my club," I said.

We ran down the hallway, past rooms filled with more debris and Zs. As we moved, they followed until they crowded the hallway behind us. Jesus Christ! The minute we ran into a dead end, we were going to be devoured.

A Z staggered out of the room ahead of me and I crushed him with the wrench. Christy turned and fired, hitting one in the chest. It didn't put him down, but it was enough to make a minor roadblock when he fell back into a mass.

Frosty nipped at a Z but kept well away. The dog was smarter than the two of us combined, with her little antics.

I grabbed a door that was lying in the hallway and wedged it between two entryways. Not a great barrier, but it would buy us a few seconds.

We rounded a corner and there were two brutes ahead. One of the Zs was probably Samoan, and his female partner was just as large.

"How many bullets?" I asked Christy.

"Two, but I have a few more in my pocket," she called back.

"Take the woman, I got the big guy."

Christy moved to my flank, set her feet and aimed. The first shot went wide.

I advanced on the guy and hoped we weren't swarmed from behind. He swung at me, so I swung back. The wrench connected with a fleshy arm and he shifted to the side. He came at me again, so I kicked at his knee and connected with a shin. It was like kicking a tree trunk.

The woman barreled into me and I hit the wall. Christy maneuvered behind me and I prayed she didn't accidentally shoot me.

I backed up a half step, swung the wrench around, and cracked it against the big guy's arm. The blow was answered by the sound of crushed bones, but it didn't even faze him.

Frosty growled and dashed between the pair. She moved down the hallway, turned and barked. The Zs turned to check out the noise.

I didn't have much left. The last swing had taken my energy reserves from around five percent to zero.

Christy shouldered me aside, stepped into a shooter's stance, and shot the woman in the head. She fell back, slapped the gun open and started to reload.

The big Z stepped on the woman and fell forward. He grabbed me as he went down, and took me to the ground. He trapped my legs under his big body and crawled toward me. He reeked of rot and old blood. What little clothing he wore was ripped and covered in gore. His mouth, coming toward my face, was all broken teeth, blue-rimmed lips, and pale gums. When they got me, I was going to be one dead squid.

The wrench was a hundred-pound barbell. I could barely lift it, and my swing was weaker than a six-year-old's. The head hit the Z and pissed him off even more.

I wedged the wrench under his chin and pushed up with both hands.

The Zs behind us stumbled over the half-assed barricade and closed on our position.

I tried to get my leg under the Z and use the maneuver Anna had performed on the shuffler the night before, but he was too heavy.

Christy saved me.

She lifted the Z's head by a clump of hair, put her revolver to his temple, and blew his brains out.

It took me precious seconds to wiggle out from under the mass. When we both staggered around the corner with a horde of fresh Zs on our ass, it was only to find the back emergency door.

I ignored the "Warning: Alarm Will Sound" sign, took a running start, and hit the door hard enough to rattle the wall. Thankfully it gave, and I crashed through and hit the ground. Christy and Frosty followed close behind, the dog coming to my side, tail wagging like she was laughing at me.

Christy acted fast and slammed the door shut. She picked up a piece of splintered wood and jammed it between the door and the frame, then kicked it until it was wedged in there tight. The Zs moaned behind the barricade, but they were stuck for now. However, the barricade wouldn't last for long.

I got to my feet and poked my head around the corner, cautious for any gunshots.

What I saw made me utter a long and well-deserved "Fuck!"

The wrecked trucks were still there and burning, but that was all. The helicopter was a blip as it sped across the sky. Whoever had been shooting at the military guys was also gone.

The battle was over.

The shapeless mass that had been advancing on the base was a little more visible now, and it was just as I'd suspected: an army of the dead, at least as large as the one we'd fled from in San Diego was moving on the base. Gunshots sounded, but the inhabitants must have become spooked, because an exodus was underway. Trucks departed at high speed, with men and women pouring out from the walls.

The place was about to be completely overrun, and we'd been left behind.

The Fuckening

09:00 hours approximate
Location: Just outside of Oceanside

I dropped to the ground and leaned my back against the apartment building wall. Zs pounded on the door, but I didn't care. We'd fought, run, escaped the odds, and now our friends were gone. Joel and Anna had left us behind. I stared up at the sky and wondered what we were supposed to do now.

Not only that, but a flood of Zs was about to overrun this entire area.

Christy grabbed my arm and tugged, but I pulled back.

"Jackson, we need to move. That door's not going to hold for very long," she pleaded.

"I know."

She stared at me, but didn't say another word. Frosty panted and watched the doorway. She sat next to me and leaned over to lick my face. I pushed her away.

I took a deep breath and got to my feet. No

sense in sitting around waiting to be devoured. If I'd learned anything, it was that finding a place to hole up--even if it was for a few hours--was more important than just about anything.

Christy took my hand, and together we moved out.

Instinct kicked in, taking all of ten seconds. Bob and weave; that was the idea. Joel used to say that you had to think about every move, think about the layout of the ground you were about to traverse. Look for places to hide, and always keep your head up and on the lookout.

But Joel was gone.

We didn't have much, besides a few weapons and our wits.

I pulled it together, stood, and struck out with my companions at my side.

We traversed a four-lane road and moved West until we'd gone a few miles--hopefully far away from the horde. We found a burned-out Albertsons, but didn't bother to poke our heads inside the building.

A strip mall sat across a parking lot, so we made for a T-Mobile store that featured broken windows, a smashed-in front door, and displays that used to feature the best of current technology. Cell phones, what a convenience they'd been. I could have picked up my phone and called Anna to find out where they'd run off to. The way Joel had been talking, he might have just decided to abandon my ass.

The employees' room was small and had been tossed, but we found a chair and managed to wedge it against the door. I was hungry. Christy was grumpy, and Frosty had gas. Somehow we managed to settle into the little room and curl up together.

"Do you think they'll come back for us?"

"I don't know. I hope they do, but we're a few miles away from the battle and they won't even know where to start looking," I replied.

We chatted for a few minutes, but weariness was heavy and I found my eyes closing.

"Want me to take first watch?" Christy asked.

"If Zs wander in here, we're dead anyway. Just get some rest," I said.

Christy didn't answer, but tears welled up in her eyes.

"I'm sorry, Christy. I feel like I let us down and now we're all alone," I said.

"We have each other and we have Frosty. She's a badass dog, you know," Christy smiled.

I smiled back.

14:00 hours approximate
Location: Just outside of Oceanside

We rose a half dozen hours later.

Night was in full swing, and my stomach grumbled about the lack of food. Christy didn't complain, but I could tell she was hungry because she kept going through the remains of an overturned desk, looking for a morsel.

I dragged the chair out of the way and opened the door in slow motion. When fifty Zs didn't fall on us, I moved into the room, my wrench held up high.

I felt a little better, rested, but every inch of my body hurt. I had bruises in crazy places, and my arms were so sore I thought I'd be good for one or two blows at most if we ran across any Zs.

We ranged out and poked around a couple of stores, but they were long since emptied. We managed to find a can of baby formula that had been left in a bag of diapers, and took it. With no water, we weren't sure how to consume it. Christy gave a half-laugh as I tried to eat a little bit, but my mouth was so dry that I coughed it back up.

We'd need to make some water filters and soon, if we wanted to survive. Rain had come and gone, leaving puddles, but we weren't about to drink anything out of a pothole.

As morning faded into afternoon, we were still on the lookout for anything resembling food or water. Christy and I found another apartment building, but it had been stripped clean a few times over, with the exception of some clothes and a couple of blankets, not to mention all the abandoned furniture, smashed glasses and broken dishes.

But Joel and I had become good at looking in weird places. I pulled a high shelf out of a closet and we found a small bag of chips that had expired a year ago.

We gathered a few more small items, consisting of a couple of mints, a Hostess Twinkie that we would have to fight to the death over, and a single Diet Coke. We kept to doorways and under the cover of strip malls as we made our way back to the T-Mobile store. After poking around and making sure that no Zs had wandered into the store during the day, I wedged the chair against the door.

Christy looked as dejected as I felt, but we passed the soda back and forth and tried to outdo each other with belches. Then Christy got a fearful look in her eyes, so we went into silent running mode again.

We ate the little bit of food, and then Christy spent an inordinate amount of time nibbling her half of the stale Twinkie, while I devoured mine in one bite.

After an hour of staring at the wall, I heard a noise in the store. Christy checked the load in her revolver, and I tried to act like I was prepared for the worst by checking my wrench.

I slid the chair aside and slowly opened the door.

It was late and night had set in. I stared into the darkness, but nothing moved. It was just as we'd seen it a few hours ago, with its overturned chairs and broken displays laying like giant skeletons. I was about to close the door when a woman's voice spoke.

"Easy, bud. No harm meant."

I stiffened. I'd heard that phrase one too many times. "No harm" usually meant that someone meant some very serious fucking harm.

Frosty growled low in her throat.

"I know that look, and I promise it's cool. We were on patrol when I noticed this place. Thought I might pick up an old cell phone, you know, like the old days. Sometimes you get one with some juice and a few tunes pre-loaded. I've gone through five or six now. The best is when you find one in someone's pocket or bag and it's filled with jams. I miss music, man. Cute dog, by the way. Hope she doesn't try to eat my face."

I didn't say a word but touched Frosty's head to reassure her.

She'd been squatting next to a pile of boxes-- stuff we'd been through and tossed aside. She stood up on creaking knees and lowered her rifle. The gun looked like something Joel Kelly would have fallen in love with.

The woman was dressed in black and wore straps and a belt, from which a number of weapons hung: a sidearm, a pair of knives, a flashlight, multiple magazines, and what looked like a canister of pepper spray. She appeared to be a little younger than me, and had a pair of big brown eyes with arched eyebrows.

"You alone?" she asked.

"We don't want any trouble, truly. We've seen

enough crazy shit over the last few weeks to last a lifetime," I said.

"We. Got it, so there's more than one. Listen, I know I look like I might be as dangerous as a flea, but I'm pretty fast with this gun. Plus, one whistle and this place will be swarming. Why don't you come out and join us? We're heading back to base, and we have hot food, water, and even a place to sleep," she said.

I swallowed back a curt "No," but my stomach grumbled loud enough to attract a couple of shufflers.

"Wait, base? You're from the military base?"

"Not those guys. Bunch of assholes trying to destroy the world, and we're trying to rebuild it. You'd think that the z-poc would bring people together, but it just made the divide even deeper. That's why we need some fresh blood. Just come on out and after we talk, I promise you that if you don't like me and my friends you can just fuck off on your way and go find a nice horde to party with."

Christy pushed past me into the room and studied the woman. She held her revolver in one hand, but it hung at her side. Frosty wandered into the room and sniffed the woman's leg.

She stayed still while the dog checked her out.

"I'm confused. We saw a battle earlier." I was careful not to show any complicity on either side. "We didn't want to get caught in the middle, so we've been in hiding. We lost our gear."

"That battle was a real fucking mess, friend. Didn't want any part of it, but they started shooting at us. We were scouting that massive horde when someone in a truck opened fire on one of our vehicles."

"Wow," I said, trying to play it cool. When we'd been heading back to base one of the military trucks had been blown half off the road. I clearly remember one of the men yelling "IED".

"It was a real clusterfuck," she said and reached down to let Frosty sniff her hand.

"So you got attacked, and then what?"

"Not much else. Returned fire, took a few losses, but that horde was closing in on the new Bright Star base, and we wanted nothing to do with a hundred thousand Zs." She slipped off a black cap and rubbed at her forehead.

"Jackson?" Christy asked.

I put my hand in hers and gripped it tight.

"I'm confused. Who are you with?"

"Easy enough, friend. They started calling us Reavers because it sounds more ominous than 'the others'. Sounds silly when you think about it, especially with us fighting to liberate cities while they are fighting to lock them down. Containment, they call it, but I call it a prison. Enough about all that stuff. Just understand that we're the good guys."

The ground rocked beneath us. I threw my hands out to grab for anything but ended up catching Christy. We both went to the ground in a heap. Frosty ran back into our little improvised room and cowered.

The woman sat down and looked, worried. No. She looked like she was about to shit bricks.

"That is not good. They're moving much faster than we'd anticipated," she said.

A roar built and passed over us taking more than a few seconds to pass. The building shook so hard I thought it was going to fall apart.

"The fuck was that?" I realized I was yelling.

"They just nuked LA. The new plan is sterilization; build on what's left after the earth's been cleansed. Never mind that it's going to poison everything with radiation. Fuckers," she said.

I shook my head at the absurdity. I helped Christy off the ground and together we moved to the door. I stepped over shattered glass and poked our heads outside.

Much to my horror, I found that the woman hadn't lied because a mushroom cloud rose far to the North.

I nodded, unable to find words, because the entire world was nuts, and we were right in the middle of The Fuckening.

This is Machinist Mate First Class Jackson Creed, and I am still alive.

THE END

The story will continue in _Z-Risen 4: Reavers_

Why I wrote *Z-Risen: Poisoned Earth*

I've written a lot of zombie books over the years and I've always had fun trying to come up with new twists in the genre. *Z-Risen* was born out of a conversation, over beers, with my friend Craig DiLouie in mid-2013. I had an idea to do a military-themed series based partially on my own time in the United States Navy, and pair up a Navy Engineer with a Marine. The two forces have always had a friendly rivalry, and I thought it would make for a good story.

The book was initially written as a free web serial, and it was set in the same world as my Permuted Press book *Beyond the Barriers*--the books can be read independently.

I'm an indie author and I work very hard on my books. I hold down a fulltime job, have a family, and still manage to get in a few hours a day to write. I love hearing input from readers, and the best way to provide that is via a review.

When you leave a review on Amazon, Barnes & Noble, Smashwords, or where ever you purchased a book, it helps other readers. This also helps the author out more than you can imagine. It's hard to be a successful independent author, but when a book sells well, it is likely to get sequels, and that's what I have planned for the *Z-Risen* series.

So please, friends, if you can spare a few minutes of your time, go and review *Z-Risen: Poisoned Earth* on Amazon.

Watch for *Z-Risen 4: Reavers* in 2015.

Read the Permuted Press novel that inspired the Z-Risen series.

BEYOND THE BARRIERS

When the dead rise, Ex-Special Forces soldier Erik Tragger flees to the mountains to wait out the end of the world. Cut off from civilization for months, he returns to find cities ruined and ruled by the walking dead.

Tragger reluctantly joins a group of survivors with a plan: flee to Portland where humanity is carving out a stronghold. But along the way they face opposition at every turn—the dead, rogue military forces, looters... and a new enemy more dangerous than any they have yet encountered.

Among the stumbling, mindless zombies walk the ghouls. The ghouls are living dead creatures that not only strategize and plan, but also possess the ability to guide their shambling brothers.

With weapons and supplies dwindling, Erik and his companions will faceoff against millions of the dead who have but one goal: complete eradication of the last of the living.

About the Author

Timothy W. Long has been writing tales and stories since he could hold a crayon and has also read enough books to choke a landfill. He has a fascination with all things zombies, a predilection for hula-girl dolls, and a deep-seated need to jot words on paper and thrust them at people.

Tim is the author of:

Beyond the Barriers (Permuted Press)
Among the Living (Permuted Press)
Among the Dead (Permuted Press)
At the Behest of the Dead
The Zombie Wilson Diaries
The Apocalypse and Satan's Glory Hole
w/ Jonathan MoOn
Dr. Spengle vs. The Unihorn Horror
w/ Jonathan MoOn
Z-Risen: Outbreak
Z-Risen: Outcasts
Z-Risen: Poisoned Earth

Coming Soon
Impact Earth: First Wave
Z-Risen 4: Reavers

http://timothywlong.com
http://www.facebook.com/TimothyWLong
@TimWLong

Made in the USA
San Bernardino, CA
14 February 2018